Killer's Cross

(A DI Shona McKenzie Mystery)

Wendy H. Jones

Gwen,

Wendy H. Jones

Published by Scott and Lawson

www.wendyhjones.com

Cover Design by Cathy Helms of Avalon Graphics LLC

ISBN: 978-0-9930677-4-7

DEDICATION

To my aunt, Moyra McDermott, who has believed in me and encouraged me every step of the way.

To my readers who have taken DI Shona McKenzie to their hearts and who make these books possible.

ACKNOWLEDGMENTS

I would like to thank the following people who have helped me in so many ways.

Anne Hawkins and Stephanie Kerr Black for their tireless work with editing.

Fellow crime author Chris Longmuir, for all her help and support throughout the process of bringing the book to completion.

Karen Wilson of Ginger Snap Images, Dundee for the professional author photographs.

Nathan Gevers for all his hard work and enthusiasm building the website for my books.

Police Scotland for their patience in answering myriad questions about the nuts and bolts of policing. Particular thanks must go to my local police sergeant who has never failed to answer any of my questions with good humour and has supported me in my endeavor.

The members of the Angus Writers Circle for their valuable advice, feedback and support

1

Lying on the damp earth, listening to the grating of a rusty lock, she knows her life is about to end. She is alone in this prison. Thick darkness, like a shroud, engulfs her body in its muffled tendrils. She bites back a scream and shouts.

"Help. Help Me."

Ineffectual, her voice fades into the inky night. She shifts her body. No comfort. She cannot move far, chained as she is. Tense muscles strain against the rapidly cooling metal. She feels pain, unimaginable pain. Her breathing quickens as panic takes hold. She forces herself to relax. To think. To take stock. Uses her mind to explore. She uses her fingers and feet to survey her surroundings. Wood, dirt floor. The dank smell of wet earth. A shed? An outhouse? A barn?

Then, a delicate tickle against her skin. Soft, gentle it travels up her bare leg prickling along every tiny nerve end. Creeping, crawling, relentless. She kicks. Tries to push it off with her hands. The chains stop her. She can't reach. It is still there. There is no escape. Another joins it. Myriad others. Spiders, her worst fear. They are all over her. Shaking, she screams then snaps her mouth shut as she feels them on her face. She is rigid. There is no way out.

She prays for death.

2

Flashing an ID card the flapper steps through the dimly lit, red brick archway towards the body of the dead vicar. It's not often you find a flapper at a crime scene. Not in Dundee anyway. Shona is the flapper, more commonly known to the good people of Dundee as, Detective Inspector Shona McKenzie. She doesn't need to look too closely at the body to know this particular vicar has not died well. His face is set in a death mask grimace, his clothes torn, and a cross has been carved on his chest.

"Hoy. Laurel and Hardy get yourselves over here." Dundee CID have been to the Tayside Police Annual Charity Ball. Not that Tayside Police exists any more but in the police, like many institutions, tradition lingers.

The pair, aka Detective Sergeant Peter Johnston and Detective Constable Iain Barrow leap to it and hurry over. "What do you make of this?" asks Shona.

"A vicar? First it's nuns and now a vicar. What's the world coming tae," says Peter.

Their last case had been awash with nuns, both dead and alive, but Shona is sure it has nothing to do with their current corpse. She is hoping so anyway. Arresting the ecclesiastical fraternity is not her favourite occupation.

"I know there's not much light but there doesn't seem to be any blood. I'd expect a lot more given the adornment on his chest. Iain can you get some photos?"

"I'm on it ma'am. I'll do what I can until Eddie

tips up with the lights."

"Is Eddie the only person who works for the council? It always seems to be him who comes to our scenes."

"He has a soft spot for you Ma'am. Being as he's the senior bloke he says he wants to be called any time you need lights. He wants to make sure you get it done right," says Peter.

"Well go Eddie. I've got a fan club. Who would have thought it? The Procurator Fiscal might get jealous though so I'm off to have a word with the POLSA." She has an initial look before she speaks to the Police Official Licenced Search Advisor

Hurrying over to Sergeant Muir, she passes Charlie Chaplin, Marilyn Munroe, and Sophia Loren. More members of her team, DC Roy MacGregor, DS Abigail Lau, and DS Nina Chakrabarti respectively. "Get the gawkers away from the wall," she calls to them. "How can there be so many people at this time of night? Tell them the cabaret is over. They're cluttering up my crime scene. Shut the street if you have to." The poor unsuspecting public doesn't stand a chance with those three on their tails, thinks Shona.

Approaching Sergeant Muir, she asks, "What's the story? Who found him?"

"The pair of drunks sitting on the grass. Went into the archway for a quickie and got more than they bargained for. It put a right damper on their ardour."

"I bet it did. Are they fit to be interviewed?"

"Not a snowballs chance. I'm surprised they remembered 999 never mind fire up enough brain cells to give you a coherent story."

"Great." Shona calls over to her team. "Abigail, take this sorry pair down to the nick. Force-feed them coffee and lots of grease. Sober them up for an interview."

As Eddie has now worked his magic with the lights Shona has a closer look at the dead vicar.

“Hi Eddie. We must stop meeting like this.”

“Aye Shona. Much as I like seeing you it would be better at a sensible time o’ the day.”

“It would that Eddie. Unfortunately the murderers don’t seem to have got the memo.”

The body doesn't look any better by the million watts light of an LED. Unkempt hair, needs a shave, not the sort of look she expects from a vicar. She bends down. He looks and smells like he hasn't had a wash in months. Badly bitten fingernails are ingrained with dirt. Despite this the clothes look clean and there are no signs of blood. None. Iain will get them into evidence so he can do some tests.

“He’s a bit scruffy for a vicar do ye no’ think ma’am. I’ve met a lot of vicars in my time, an’ I know some o’ the more modern ones can be a bit casual, but no’ as bad as this.”

“English please Peter. I’ve enough on my plate interpreting a crime scene without doing the same with your speech.”

“Aye ma’am. Sorry.” He doesn't look particularly sorry. This probably has something to do with the large grin on his face. Peter doesn't give a toss what Shona, or anyone else, thinks of his accent.

“You seem to be akin to the Oracle of Delphi when it comes to all things Dundee. Do you know where this particular vicar hangs up his Theology Certificate?”

“Not a clue. I can honestly say I’ve never clapped eyes on him before in my life. I’d remember a vicar carrying that particular odour.”

“Do you know who the vicar is here?”

“No’ now. It used to belong to the Catholics but its been taken over by some trendy lot.”

“I’ll pin it down when I get back to the office. It

shouldn't be that hard. The Gateway is fairly well known and it'll be all over the Internet." She looks around. "I haven't seen hide nor hair of Soldier Boy yet. Find out where he is. You and Nina take one of the boys each and search the area. If you haven't got torches in your cars then borrow them from all the uniform cops who are milling around." Soldier Boy is DC Jason Roberts, one of the newest members of her team. Jason got his nickname as he'd done a stint in the TA before joining the police. This had come in very useful in their last two big cases. There seem to be rather a lot of murders in Dundee. This might be why it is known as the murder capital of Scotland.

As Peter leaves, Shona turns to examine the corpse. She bends down to see if he has any ID in his pockets. He doesn't even have any pockets so no help there. The singular lack of blood bothers her. He's obviously been murdered elsewhere and carried here, but surely there should be blood on his clothes or around the large cross adorning his chest. She is interrupted by a gravelly voice that she recognises instantly. It sends her nerve ends dancing with excitement. It belongs to the Procurator Fiscal, Douglas Lawson, who also happens to be her boyfriend. She turns as he says, "Hi Shona. Here we go again. Dating over dead bodies." His eyes are blue and sparkle with laughter. These and his smile make Shona come over all peculiar. She must be the only woman in the history of Christendom whose love life is carried out at crime scenes.

She manages to calm down and keep a professional yet friendly manner. She's sure it doesn't fool the Procurator Fiscal one bit. "Douglas. This is a strange one even for me. A dead vicar with a huge cross carved on his chest. Given that, I think we can safely say he was murdered. Unless Burke and Hare have resurrected themselves and moved to Dundee."

"With you involved nothing would surprise me," he replies.

Larry Briar, the police surgeon, interrupts them. Having been at the same party as the rest of them, he is dressed as a police surgeon from the 1920's. Larry may be excellent at his job but he is sadly lacking in imagination.

"Shona, how did I know that I wouldn't be able to get through a night out in your company, without being called to a murder?"

Given the amount of murders that have happened on her watch she has the reputation of being the grim reaper of Dundee. She's given up trying to defend herself. It's easier.

"It won't take you long to certify this one, but I'd like your thoughts when you're done."

Douglas and Shona step back to let him through the archway. It takes him under a minute.

"Agreed and certified. That's the most bloodless murder scene I've attended in 30 years in the job." He is wiping sweat from his brow with a large spotted hankie. "Warm isn't it?"

During her time in Dundee Shona has come to realise that Dundonians always have to mention the weather. It's a national pastime.

"Mary will love this one," he says.

Mary is the pathologist for the area and Shona has to agree, she does like a puzzle. He leaves and Douglas says he has to follow suit.

"I've left Rory and Alice in the tender care of my brother in law. I'd better not stretch his willingness too far as I dragged him out of bed. He came across in his PJ's."

"I'm surprised Rory's not here with you." Douglas's ten-year-old son is fascinated with Shona's job and has a habit of appearing beside her corpses. She realises that is weird, but everyone who meets her soon comes to know that her working life closely resembles an episode of the Three Stooges. Nothing ever goes to plan. Restraining the urge to kiss him, she says goodbye. Kissing beside a dead body is too way out even for her. Some people would also consider it unprofessional.

Iain has finished processing the crime scene, so she leaves the POLSA and his team to guard the body until the mortuary collects it. The Chief is still at the party, dressed as Attila the Hun, so she takes out her iPhone to give him an update. When she finishes telling him about a corpse with a cross carved in its chest and a blood free crime scene, there is silence. She waits.

"Am I ever going to get an evening out without you spoiling it with tales of murder. This one is extraordinary even for you. Start the investigation and ring me in the morning. Late morning or my wife is not going to be best pleased."

She opens her mouth to reply but is stopped dead by the dial tone. Nothing new then. Here we go with his bally wife again. Why have I always got to run my investigations to the whims of the Chief's iron fisted wife she wonders? Shoving aside thoughts of carving hooray into the Chief's dead body she finds the team to let them know she is off back to the station.

"How come you always get to go to the office and we're left slaving over a crime scene?" says Roy.

"It's one of the perks of being a DI. Persecuting you is one of my favourites." When she first met Roy she would have torn a strip off him for this. She and DC MacGregor didn't get off to the best of starts. However, he is less like a sulky child these days. More like a spaniel - bouncy, naughty and grows on you. She is liable to give him the benefit of the doubt and he is shaping up to be a fairly useful member of the team.

Back at the office she switches on the coffee machine and adds a rich Brazilian blend that she has brought in. As it is now 3 a.m., and she has been up since the previous morning, the zip-a-dee part of her doo dah day has long gone. She is pinning her hopes on the fact that copious amounts of coffee might haul at least the zip part back.

Abigail is in the office drinking Chinese Tea. Shona's never seen the benefits of the beverage but as Abigail is Chinese she can wax lyrical about it all day. A bit like the Scots and whisky. Talking of whisky, Shona is glad she was driving and had only one glass before being pulled out of the ball. Hangovers, and crime scenes do not make for an easy partnership.

"How are the drunks? Capable of being interviewed?"

"Not a chance. They're snoring their heads off in separate cells."

"What on earth did you charge them with? As far as we know they haven't done anything other than be in the wrong place at the wrong time."

"Nothing. I've just given them bed and board for the night. That way they'll be here, if not exactly ready and waiting, in the morning."

"Good grief woman. Wait until the Chief hears that we're using his cells as a doss house."

"We won't tell him then, ma'am."

Shona grins. "Good plan. I like the way you think. Were you as bad as this in the Highlands and Islands?" Abigail transferred to Shona's team before their last big case. She is a real asset.

"Much worse ma'am. You're getting off lightly."

"I'd hate to see you at your peak. Is someone keeping an eye on them in case they choke on their own vomit?"

"All in hand ma'am. They'll be suffering from no more than a headache and a severe case of regret in the morning."

"Thanks. Get it written up and we'll speak when the others appear."

Leaving Abigail to her tea and paperwork Shona grabs her coffee and fires up the computer. They've recently been issued with Apple iMacs so she is up and running in no time. They also had new furniture a few months back. Shona managed to sneak 'top of the range' past the Chief so her desk is as fancy as the iMac. He hadn't been a happy chappy when he'd found out but by then it was too late. Luckily she was at the blazing centre of an explosive murder enquiry at the time so she couldn't be fired. Good job really or she would now be working in McDonalds. She straightens a pencil on her pristine desk. Just the way she likes it.

She soon has all the details on the newly appointed vicar at the Gateway. Or should she say Pastor. Google informs her it is one Ms Candace Sanchez of the Dundee International Pentecostal Church of Christ. The church has an emergency contact number and she sets about ruining Ms Sanchez's beauty sleep. She thinks about leaving it but doesn't want the Pastor to tip up at the church unawares. Also, one of the gawkers might have been a concerned parishioner who could deliver the news before the police. Ms Sanchez is obviously used to being woken up in the middle of the night, as the early morning call doesn't seem to faze her. She agrees to come to the station and talk to them. Shona is hoping that the woman might know the identity of the dead vicar.

The Pastor turns up before most of the team, which gives Abigail and Shona a chance to interview her. In her late twenties and casually dressed she is definitely an improvement on the last pair Shona and Abigail had interviewed together - Russian twins who were right up to their thick Slavik necks in nefarious goings on. Violence was written into their DNA so it had not been a pleasant experience.

She spouts the preliminaries for the benefit of the recording, "Interview with Ms Candace Sanchez. DI Shona McKenzie and DS Abigail Lau in attendance. Ms Sanchez, are you the Pastor of Dundee International Pentecostal Church of Christ?"

"Yes I am, but only for the past few weeks." Her accent is pure bred Southern American.

Thankfully Iain has returned to the fold so Shona passes a digital photograph across the table. Face photo only. She doesn't want to give any of the facts of the case away.

"Do you know this man?"

"Not that I'm aware of. He doesn't look familiar."

"You haven't seen him at any Ecumenical Meetings."

"I haven't been to any yet. I've only been in the UK for six weeks and this is my first Pastorate."

"Could he be a member of your congregation?"

"Definitely not. It's only been going for about a year so it's still small. Nine of the members came from the States with me, so I know everyone."

This is getting them nowhere. Shona decides to leave it there and do a round of all the churches in Dundee in the morning. That will be fun she thinks. Dundee has a lot of churches.

"Thank you Ms Sanchez. We'll be in touch if we need anything else."

"Can I get into my church?"

"Not through that door but through any other door you want. It looks like the church is sealed up tight so you won't be disturbing any evidence inside."

When the team return they congregate in the still immaculate incident room. It won't be long before it looks like the wreck of the Hesperus. All the information gathered in the course of an investigation tends to clutter the place up. Shona switches on a fan. Larry was right. It is warm. Dundee is in the middle of a heat wave and it's looking like it will be a scorcher in the morning. The concrete monstrosity that is Bell St Station could neither keep them warm in the winter, nor cool in the summer. It is hell on earth either way.

"What did you find?" asks Shona.

Peter takes the lead. "Nothing important. The usual beer cans and used condoms round the back of the church. The front is well cared for and there were only a couple of bottles, which had been chucked across the wall. In the light of day we'll need to look in the skips. I've earmarked Roy and Jason for that little job."

Shona sees Roy's mouth open and forestalls him. "Don't even think about saying that we're picking on the men here Roy. This is not a feminist thing, you guys just happen to be the tallest." His mouth snaps shut. In the past Roy has had a bee in his bonnet, which was almost akin to racism and sexism, but this had been stamped on and he has been fine since. She doesn't want it to rear its ugly head again. Roy needs a tight leash to keep him on the straight and narrow.

"We'll be back on it first thing tomorrow, or should I say later today. Off you go and get a few hours sleep. I'll see you all back here at 0900." Even Nina, the original party animal is up and running. If any of their previous cases were anything to go by, they have a long, and tiring, haul ahead of them. As Shona drives home to her bed, and Shakespeare her cat, she has a feeling in every bone she possesses that this is another case which will not be easy.

3

Most of Shona's previous cases found her being woken by an early morning phone call. Thankfully this one lets her lie in until the alarm goes off at 0730. She staggers into the kitchen and switches on the super deluxe Tassimo coffee machine. Knowing about her coffee habit and her strange working hours, her mother had given it to her a couple of Christmases ago. Shona could have elevated her to sainthood for the gift. Shakespeare is maiowing loudly that she is about to expire from hunger and what is Shona going to do about it. She gives the cat some gourmet lamb stuff and tries to work out if a lukewarm shower will waken her. This proves to be a cold shower day. Her brain cells need jump starting. Pouring her coffee into a thermal cup she is out the door and into the sunlight. She was right about the heat index. It is already 24 degrees and the day hasn't got going yet. Still, being somewhat of a hothouse plant, she is in her element.

Amazingly Peter has beat her to it and is starting the day with a mug of builders brew tea and... "Peter, what on earth is that? It doesn't look anything like a bacon sandwich."

"That's because it's Muesli." He stirs it around a bit and peers at it. "At least I think it's Muesli."

"Why are you eating Muesli when I've never seen you even glance in the direction of a bowl of cereal before."

"The missus has got me on a diet."

It's not often Shona is lost for words but even she takes pause at that. "A diet? Do you even know what the word means?"

"She says I'm too fat. How could she think that? There's nothing wrong with my figure."

Shona agrees with his wife but who is she to pass judgement on the corpulent physique of her senior sergeant.

"I'm afraid I can't argue with your wife Peter. If she says you're on a diet then a diet it is. If I see anything remotely resembling a calorie pass your lips then I'm reporting you. I don't want to get on the wrong side of Mrs Johnston. I value my life too much."

Peter looks even gloomier if that were possible. Nina arrives, takes one look at Peter and says, "What's up with him?"

Shona waves her flat hand in front of her throat in a go no further gesture. "Best not to ask. But no bacon rolls for us this morning. We're supporting Peter."

The rest of the team arrive and start grumbling at the news. "Stop moaning. We're all on a fitness drive. Take your stomachs into the briefing room and I'll keep you too busy to worry about your hunger." She has to admit to thinking longingly of one of Doreen's bacon rolls herself. Not that she's going to let this miserable lot know.

They are looking more like a well-oiled professional team this morning rather than a bunch of vaudeville music hall artists. Apart from Peter that is, who still manages to look like a bag of rags in his working attire, suit, shirt and tie. Roy and Nina are, as always, dressed in the latest designer gear. Shona has learned not to ask too many questions about the origins of these items. She might not want to know the answer.

"Jason, and Roy you're on skip duty as we said last night. Wear overalls, thick gloves and masks. Don't take risks. Iain you go with them and bag any evidence."

Resigned to their fate they get up and go to find all the equipment. Even Roy is quiet. Shona can see his impressive computer brain thinking about his clothes and what might happen to the Calvin Klein jeans he is sporting. The stupid sod should have thought about that when he got dressed this morning, thinks Shona.

"Peter and Abigail, get a print out of all the names and addresses of every church in Dundee and the surrounding area. Nina, you and I are going to interview our witnesses."

The drunks, who turn out to be Bella Jameson and Archie Dougal, don't actually know each other. They'd hooked up the night before and had decided they were soul mates. Hence the trip to the archway of the Gateway to seal the deal. They interview Bella first. She is a sorry sight with smudged makeup, red eyes and smelling like a nightclub the morning after. She is also at the weepy stage.

"I didnae do nothing. We just found him there."

"What time?" asks Shona.

"I don't know. I swear I don't know nothing. I cannae remember anything."

"I've a dead body on my hands and so far you and lover boy are the only people who saw him. Why should I believe you?"

"We were too drunk to do anything."

"Did you touch him?"

"No way. Why would I touch him? He was dead." A shudder ripples through her body and she bursts into tears.

Nina hands her a couple of tissues as Shona continues. "How did you know he was dead?"

Through sniffles she said, "I don't know, he just

looked dead. Archie phoned the Polis. I can't get the sight o' that cross out of my head."

"How could you see the cross? It was pitch black."

"Archie was using his phone as a torch?" She snivels and wipes her running nose.

"Did you see anyone or anything else?"

"No. Honest. I can't tell you anything."

Shona is beginning to believe her. She has the feeling they are wasting their time. She asks the poor woman to give them her address and lets her and her misery go home.

"I think she's a strawberry short of a pot of jam that one. Go get Archie and see what we can get from him."

Archie's interview continues in much the same vein but with more colourful language. The pair of them are living, breathing stereotypes of drunks, Bella weeping and Archie obstreperous.

He is dragged into the interview kicking, screaming and shouting obscenities, with an accent so thick the swear words are the only ones Shona understands. If he doesn't watch out she'll be chucking him in a cell for real. Somehow he'd managed to cut his hand in the process.

When he'd been thrown into a chair she says, "We'll find a sticking plaster for that cut of yours. It's a shame we can't stick one over your gob."

"Cheeky c—"

"That'll be enough from you. Keep a civil tongue in your mouth and treat the DI with respect."

"What would I want to do that for?"

"Because I say so." Shona is fed up with Archie already. "Around here my word is law. Now unless I or the sergeant here ask you a question keep your trap shut."

"Why would I listen tae a woman?"

Shona puts her face close to his, quite valiantly given his state of intoxication, and says, "One more word from you, unless it's to answer a question, and I'll arrest you."

He opens his mouth to speak.

"Don't even try to test me."

He very wisely decides to close his mouth and cooperate.

With Nina interpreting his broad Dundonian for Shona they get through the interview and she sends him on his merry way.

"I've never been so glad to see the back of someone in my life."

"Thank goodness we're out of there. I feel drunk on the fumes alone," says Nina. Shona echoes her sentiments. Whisky distilleries spring to mind when considering their ordeal in the interview room.

Considering the official line is that the UK is a post-Christian nation, there are a lot of churches in Dundee. Even splitting the number with Peter and Abigail, Nina and Shona find themselves talking to a great deal of people in their round of the clergy. Entering churches and cathedrals on the spectrum from inspiring to decrepit, they have the same answer at them all. No one knows of a vicar who looks anything like their dead man. Steve Garret, the minister at the Steeple, says he looks vaguely familiar.

"Do you recognise him from any of the Dundee Churches Together Meetings?" asks Shona.

"No. He's definitely not a minister. If he were then I would know. Dundee isn't that big and we all tend to know each other."

The most they can do is leave a photo with each of the Pastors, Vicars, Ministers, Priests or anything else they are called. They all say they will ask around and get back to them if they find out.

Slogging round in temperatures of 27 degrees is weary work. Although they are both dressed for the heat they discover that fashion sandals are not the best footwear for schlepping around the uneven pavements and frequent slopes of Dundee. Footsore and weary they return to the nest. Peter and Abigail look just as frazzled.

"How can there be so many clergy in such a wee city. I'm too old for all this trailing around." Lack of good food and too much exercise means Peter is not in the best of moods. His default setting is moaning, but he is much worse with his current calorie intake, or lack of calorie intake Shona supposes.

"Did you come up with anything?"

"Blisters."

"Stop whining Peter. You're a policeman, not a ballerina. Did you come up with anybody who knew our victim?"

"Not a b..., blasted soul." The team, including Peter, try to mind their P's and Q's around Shona. She doesn't tolerate bad language and on the whole they tend to respect that. He continues, "We seem to have spoken to every Christian denomination in the world, including the nuns up at the convent. They weren't very pleased to see us again."

This is hardly surprising given their last case. The inhabitants of the convent are not very fond of Police Scotland anymore and the team have been firmly struck off the their Christmas card list. Not that Shona blames them. She thinks they are actually a nice bunch and is saddened that she'd had to look into their affairs.

"Now we're in the middle of another investigation which involves the religious faithful of Dundee. I can hear Police persecution of Christians being hollered from the steeples and spires and we haven't even started. Let's hope this is an isolated incident," says Shona.

Nina bursts out laughing and says, "With your track record that's highly unlikely. You don't do simple."

"Keep your thoughts to yourself Nina and don't be so cheeky." It is said without rancour. After a couple of years they are all settling in as a team and starting to relax around each other.

"How did the skip search go boys?" The pungent whiff coming from their direction gives her the answer.

"Smelly, boring and nothing to report. That church doesn't half create a lot of rubbish," says Iain.

"It would do. The Gateway hires out its hall for functions. There's something on there nearly every day. Not only that, the new lot that took over the building from the Catholics are a pretty social bunch themselves. They had a fete on recently."

What Peter doesn't know about Dundee isn't worth knowing. Shona is pleased to have him on her team. She realises Roy and Jason are quiet, which is unusual for them.

"What's up with you pair?" They both open their mouths to speak,

"He—"

"I—" said simultaneously. Shona cuts them off at the source.

"Listen here Tweedledum and Tweedledee. Whatever you're arguing about now, it stops here. Shake hands, play nice, and forget your differences. I don't care what it's about so don't even bother trying to tell me."

Roy and Jason have the ability to rub each other up the wrong way. They have settled down a lot, and seem to be fairly friendly, but occasionally it flares up. Shona is giving them the benefit of the doubt today. Given that they'd all had about 10 minutes sleep last night everyone is frazzled and tempers are frayed.

Jason says, "Sorry ma'am. I just wanted to tell you I managed to stick myself with a used needle. It's in an evidence bag. I need to take it to the doctor and report it." Jason is the most accident-prone copper Shona has ever come across, but this is a new high even for him. No wonder the poor lad is looking grim.

"Is this anything to do with what you and Roy were arguing about?"

"No ma'am. It wasn't Roy's fault."

"Good. If you've nothing to report here go and see the doctor and get the process started. Fill out an accident report as well."

As he leaves she says, "Was there anything else in the bins?"

"Nothing that would help us ma'am," says Roy.

"It looks like we're no further forward. Time to go home methinks. You need a shower," she indicates Roy. Iain of course is fine, having only been bagging evidence. "Roy, I want a word with you before you go."

Peter is off out the door in a flash, his feet miraculously having recovered from their perilous state only moments before. Must be something to do with all the churches he's visited thinks Shona.

Back in her office she says to Roy, "You and Jason need to stop this endless bickering. You've improved dramatically over the last couple of years and I don't want it starting again. Given that he's probably worried sick about the needle stick injury he's going to be more sensitive. Keep your cool and look out for him."

"Yes Ma'am. I'm sorry. I'll make sure he's okay."

"Thanks. Off you go home. I'll see you here bright and breezy in the morning." Things have definitely improved. Even a year ago Roy would have had a full scale argument with her and told Jason to sod off.

They'd even had physical fisticuffs once in the middle of the office. He's matured a bit since then and is definitely growing up and Shona is glad. His technological expertise is legendary making him a real asset to the team. She had once thought of sending him back to uniform preferably in a city as far away from her as possible, but he was given a stay of execution.

Going back to her office she bangs into the Chief who is ready to go home. Despite the heat, he is still dressed in sartorial style in a three-piece suit, shirt and tie. He does look rather red with a patina of sweat adorning his upper lip. At least he doesn't have his customary overcoat on as a nod to the summer.

"Have you found out who the vicar is yet?"

"No sir. We've spoken to all the religious denominations and none of them are laying claim to him."

"You'd better widen the area and check Angus and Fife. Don't go repeating your previous idiocy and arrest fine upstanding members of the religious community."

"I'll try not to Sir." What did the old goat expect? She's investigating the death of a vicar. It is highly likely that she might have to interview a few Pastors in the course of her duty. She shoves away feelings, deep down inside her, that he'd look good dead in a vicar's outfit, and wishes him a warm and pleasant good night.

The look on his face says he thinks she is up to something. He obviously can't work out quite what as he turns and walks down the corridor without saying another word.

It isn't until she dismisses them all and is back in her office she realises no one has updated HOLMES the Home Office Large or Major Enquiry System. Picking up the phone she asks if PC Brian Gevers is in the office or out on the beat. He was really helpful in their last case and is a sound officer. She would like him in her team one day. It turns out he is not only in, but ready, willing and able.

"Nice to see you again ma'am. Are you swimming in dead bodies again?"

"More like paddling Brian. We've only one this time."

"I'm sure you'll manage to change that before long." Even the newest members of the force feel they have something to say about Shona's reputation.

"How's that scooter of yours going? Running well?" Not that she knows anything about scooters but the rest of her team seem to think his is the business as the saying goes.

"Sweet as, ma'am."

The preliminaries over she sits him down at a spare computer and lets him loose on HOLMES. "Let's see if our modern day Sherlock can help us."

Three weary hours later finds her heating up the meal which her Grandmother has kindly provided. Before you think her granny is one of those old ladies who dispense tea and sympathy, lets put the record straight. She has just returned from an adult gap year, or actually two years. She's spent that time touring the world including trekking in Nepal and a trip to Machu Pichu. From her Facebook pictures and tweets it would appear she had visited every country in the world, including, inexplicably, both North and South Korea. Shona thinks only her dear old granny could manage that little feat. She'd obviously done some cooking lessons along the way for which Shona is grateful. She is heating up a lovely Nepalese curry, which granny had said was made from goat. Shona thinks she misheard her. Where on earth would she find goat meat in Dundee? Shakespeare turns up her nose at both the goat and the remains of the gourmet lamb. It turns out she fancies fish. She must be the most pampered moggie in history, including the cat gods of ancient Egypt.

Shona considers ringing Douglas and chatting about her day. That is as far as it goes. Even the thought of his mellow voice and laughing eyes can't keep her own eyes open. She falls into bed and sleeps as though drugged.

4

Shona awakens from a dream where a giant lobster is being chased by a llama that roars like a lion. Not a moment too soon. The lobster is just about to catch her in its pincers. She is soaked in sweat, and Shakespeare, purring loudly, is kneading her chest and breathing a foul fishy smell over her. I seriously need to stop eating so much cheese late at night she thinks. Shakespeare's breath isn't the only thing to smell ripe. She didn't even have the energy to brush and floss before collapsing in bed. That shows the extent of her exhaustion. She's usually fastidious, almost to the point of OCD.

Shona is the first one in. She considers this a bit slap dash of the others given she was the last man standing the night before.

Peter arrives first. "Where is everyone? Have you sent them out canvassing in the country? I'm no' that late."

"Your guess is as good as mine. You'd think I'd given them all the day off."

It isn't long before they all arrive, each one looking worse than the last. Nina, as always, seems to be the only one who has one iota of vim and vigour.

"Either you lot have all caught the flu or Nina dragged you down the pub last night."

"Your second guess is right. Not only that she had us drinking Gin and Slim," said Abigail.

"Gin and Slim? What on earth for."

"She said we couldn't drink pints, out of solidarity

with Peter and his diet."

"Dinnae drag me into this. I was at home eating the fat free dinner the wife cooked, not gallivanting with you lot."

"I've no sympathy for any of you. You should know by now that Nina can drink you all under the table. What time were you drinking until?"

"We weren't late ma'am. Only 2300." Nina is cheerful.

"Go and get yourselves some coffee and extra strong mints. Be quick about it. We've a full day ahead of us. Nina, I want a word with you." The others leave.

"Nina, you're a bad influence. Stop leading them astray. I need them fully alert and standing tall with some measure of energy."

She laughs. "You've got it Shona. I'll be a perfect angel."

Experience has taught Shona not to believe a word Nina says. Still her laughter is infectious and Shona finds herself joining in.

"I was trying to cheer Jason up. He looks like someone's just killed his firstborn, and for good reason."

"Good idea, but keep them in one piece next time."

"What's with the posh frock? Are you trying to impress a vicar? Gone off the Procurator Fiscal have we."

"Don't be so blasted cheeky. Go rally the troops Sergeant Chakrabarti. I've an investigation to run. The posh frock, as you so delicately put it, is in honour of the Sahara Desert like temperatures Dundee seems to be managing to muster up."

The team look a little less like hung over highland coos, with some coffee inside them. Shona suspects they've also managed to secretly scarf down a bacon roll or two but she isn't going to enquire too closely.

Not that it has anything to do with her, but she doesn't want Peter falling off the wagon. His wife can be a right mama bear where her family is concerned. The hours Shona has Peter working, she needs Mrs Johnston on side.

"Despite your obvious fragility I still need you to hot foot it round the churches in the highways and byways of the further reaches of our patch. Roy, you're on computer duty." She pauses as she sees Roy's face. "Don't look so smug. You're going to be chained to your desk. Peter, you're with me, we'll take Montrose and the surrounding area. Nina and Jason, you're on Blairgowrie and it's immediate environs. Abigail and Iain take Fife."

They groan. "Stop whining. It's your own fault. Drink lots of water and you'll be fine. Get a list of the first few churches from Roy. He'll then email you with updated lists throughout the day, so make sure your phones are on. Hop to it and go investigate."

Peter seems to have regained his equilibrium and is in fine fettle on the drive to Montrose. With the sun sending shimmering waves bouncing off the tarmac, and the window down, it feels good to be alive thinks Shona. They take the back roads to Montrose through countryside so beautiful it can make a body's heart swell with pride at being Scottish. Shona is sure other nations feel exactly the same, but the Scots are certainly proud of their country. It is easy to see why on their journey. It is marred slightly by the smell of manure and pig pens, but the pair take this minor inconvenience in their stride. Arriving in Montrose they stroll along the street licking an ice cream cone. A small one in Peter's case and imagination can only dream up the size of Shona's. Sufficient to say it dwarfs Peter's. He takes it fairly magnanimously considering.

"Do ye think we're likely to pin down the identity of the poor soul who ended up on the Gateway's doorstep?" Peter wipes away the strawberry ice cream, which is dribbling down his chin. In usual Peter fashion some is now adorning his previously fairly clean tie.

"Not a chance in hell I would say. At least we're having a pleasant afternoon away from the salt mines."

They pass a beggar in the street and Shona gives him a fiver.

"You'll be in bother doing that. We're meant to move them on," says Peter.

"I know. It's too hot to be remonstrating with anyone. Plus he belongs to Montrose so nothing to do with us."

"For a tough DI you seem to do the oddest things. Anyone would think you had a heart."

They both grin.

"Our secret Peter. I feel like I'm on holiday wandering about a strange town with an ice cream in my hand. Plus I've been asked to do a random act of kindness in memory of my friend's daughter who died about a month ago."

"I'm sorry to hear that Ma'am."

A moment later they are both transfixed by the sight of a shirtless man. His huge beer belly is hanging over a pair of low slung shorts.

"Would you look at that," says Peter. "Fifty shades o' peely wally."

"The thing's you see when you don't have a gun."

"Shall we arrest him for indecency?"

"Unfortunately I don't think beer-bellies count towards that particular law."

The man is allowed to continue on his way.

They approach the magnificent four hundred year old frontage of the Old and St Andrews Church. The sun shows it off in all it's beautiful sandstone glory, a monument to builders, and worshipers, long gone. It is situated in the equally old High Street of the town. The minister is in his office and offers them a cold drink, which they gratefully accept. They leave feeling refreshed, and much cooler, but no further forward.

"I know practically every minister in Angus after having served here for about 100 years. I can honestly say he doesn't minister at a Parish in the county."

The vicar says he is attending an ecumenical meeting the next day and agrees to pass around pictures of their dead man. It is looking highly likely he is not a man of the cloth and, like them, may have been at a fancy dress party. They leave the beautiful town behind and wend their way back to the Gulags.

They decide to delay the delights of Bell Street Station for a couple of hours and visit the fancy dress shops in Dundee. Following this they are still as ignorant. No one has hired out any vicars' costumes, only 20's costumes, all of which had been hired by the police. This case is weird, thinks Shona. With her track record she has come to expect weird.

"I'm feeling antsy. There's nothing for us to get our teeth into in this case."

"I know what you mean Ma'am. Maybe the others have found something out. All we've found is a suntan."

"Well be thankful for small mercies, at least we look healthy. I wonder how the others are faring after their heavy night?" They both grin.

They find out soon enough as the first lot appear.

"I've never been in so many churches in all my life," says Nina. "As a good Sikh I shouldn't be inside all these Christian establishments."

"A good Sikh! Are you having a giraffe? You drink more alcohol than the rest of us put together and you're at the hairdressers every week."

Nina, bursts out laughing. "You've got me there. Plus I went to the high school. We couldn't move without being dragged to a church service. There do seem to be a veritable host of churches in our wee part of Scotland though."

"Stop complaining. Did you find anything?"

"Nichego. Zilch. Most of the churches were in the middle of nowhere and I can't imagine who attends them. If our dead vicar is the incumbent at one of those I swear we wont manage to identify him until Christmas."

"Why are you speaking Russian? There's not a Russian to be seen in this case." In their previous case every time they turned around they were falling over Russians, and their nefarious goings on.

"Not yet but I'm sure it won't be long before they're somewhere in the middle of our murder. Them and Pa Broon of course."

Pa Broon is a 'pet name' for ex Lord Provost George Brown, the biggest hoodlum in the city. Shona can't seem to shake him off either. He's like a leach, only less welcome.

"Shut up Nina. I don't want that statement becoming some sort of self-fulfilling prophecy. Get Abigail on the phone and tell her and the boys to come back. They must have done Fife to death by now."

It turns out they have managed to cover the major areas of Fife between them but not a soul laid claim to their body.

"Maybe it's time to get his photograph in the press," says Shona. "Not that I really want to involve the press." In the past reporters seemed to feature rather heavily in her investigations, and not in a good way.

When everyone is back in the fold they examine the

areas they've covered.

"How large an area is left?" asks Jason, his voice flat.

"It doesn't take the brains of Einstein to work it out. Do the maths," says Roy.

"It certainly wouldn't need brains if you've worked it out. I don't think you've a grey cell between those lugs of yours. Don't be so hard on the laddie. He's not having a good week."

"Sorry. I was only joking."

"Keep your jokes to yourself Roy. They're not funny," says Shona. "Has anyone got any clue as to where we go next?"

"What about homes for retired vicars," asks Jason.

"Good one although he doesn't look very old."

"What about Carseview, the psyche unit," adds Nina.

"That's worth a try. It won't be the first time a psyche patient has had religious delusions. Give them a ring and arrange for me to go up there. I'll go and see Mary at the mortuary as well."

She could have sent one of the others to chat to the staff at Carseview but she needs to get out of her overheated office. A furnace could don its fur coat and still struggle to reach the temperature of her cubbyhole. She imagines this must be what hell is like and makes a mental note to make sure she goes to heaven.

She leaves via the boss's office to ask if she can get a warrant? "Just in case the staff wont divulge information."

"Honestly Shona, don't tell me your off to arrest a load of Psychiatric staff. That's up there with the nuns." He pauses. "You're not armed are you?"

"Of course not sir. What do you take me for? I'm just going to quietly go and ask the staff some questions."

"Don't play the innocent with me McKenzie. You always seem to be running about the streets of my city with a gun somewhere about your person. Go and conduct the investigation without causing me any problems."

"Yes Sir." There isn't much more to say, especially since the Chief is now studiously ignoring her. She'd like a gun about her person if she met him in a dark alley.

5

The trip to Carseview is a waste of time as far as the investigation goes. It is a triumph in other ways. The fact that they have air conditioning means Shona conducts an extremely thorough investigation and interviews everyone she passes, including the tea lady and the cleaners. She is seriously tempted to interview the therapy dog, which is doing the rounds of the hospital, and all the visitors, but thinks that is taking it a bit too far.

Initially they are reluctant to talk.

"We can't break patient confidentiality," says the nurse in charge.

"Even if he was a patient of yours he isn't any more. He's a dead body so I think that supersedes your code of conduct."

After that, although still not happy, they agree to look at the picture. Net result, no one knows him. Shona can't believe they are having this much trouble identifying someone in Dundee. It has been described as the largest village in the world. Everyone knows everyone, and everything about him or her. You can't keep a secret in Dundee if you are the only person who knows it and are locked in a vault.

By the time she arrives at the mortuary she is once more sporting the bedraggled sweaty look. In comparison all 4 foot 8 inches of Mary look as cool and professional as it always does. Probably something to do with the freezing cold temperatures she has to maintain to do her job. Shona thinks longingly of moving her office there until the heat wave is over.

"Afternoon Shona. Good to see you. I'm glad you're here as I was going to be ringing you anyway."

"Have you got something for me?"

"I most certainly do. You'll love this one." Mary pauses.

"Don't keep me in suspense."

"The reason there is no blood anywhere around the wound is because most of the blood has been drained from the body."

Shona takes this in, open mouthed. "What? How?" She can't drag up another word.

"Even I don't know how. I can tell you however, that you're dealing with a very smart killer. I'd say they would have had to have had training of some description."

"Why would anyone with that level of intelligence be murdering vicars and acting like a modern day vampire? This is Dundee not Transylvania."

"I agree it is bizarre. Even for you. I'm going to contact several colleagues and do some research."

"Maybe he's a doctor? Surely if there's a rogue doctor we should be able to pin him, or her, down fairly easily."

"You would think so. I've a body awaiting my tender ministrations so I'd better go. I'll be in touch if I hear anything."

On her return to the station she pops into the squad room to tell the troops she wants them in the briefing room in ten minutes. The team, hard at work, don't even look up. Shona thinks it's a bit suspicious. What are they up to? She soon finds out. Entering her office she stops dead. A humongous pot plant sits in the middle of her otherwise pristine desk. Hearing laughter she whirls round. "Who put that, that..." She is lost for words and can only manage, "there?"

"It was Mo, the cleaner," says Peter. "She decided Shona 'The Plant Killer' McKenzie needed it to cheer up her office." He takes off his glasses and wipes the tears that are running down his face.

"Cheer it up. It's like the *Day of the Triffids* in here. Who likes plants?"

Through guffaws of laughter Roy manages to choke out, "Me."

Ramming aside her astonishment, she says, "You're promoted to head gardener. Shove it on top of the filing cabinet and for goodness sake keep it alive. I don't want to get on the wrong side of Mo. Give it some water or something before it dies of heat exhaustion."

Gathered in the conference room she drops the bombshell about the bloodless corpse.

A moment of silence and then Peter says, "Since you arrived there's never been a dull minute. I thought I'd seen and heard everything on my time on the force but this takes the whole tin of biscuits."

"How do you drain blood from a human body? I just can't imagine it," says Iain.

"Do you attract eccentric murders or something?" adds Nina. "If I didn't know you any better I'd say you were doing all this yourself for fame and glory."

"Dracula does Dundee. It would make a good movie," says Roy.

"Everyone's a comedian. In the meantime we've a dead man of the cloth on our hands and no one seems to know who he is. Iain what about his finger prints."

"I managed to get a cracking set of prints but nothings come up. I've run it through all the main databases and he's not registering anywhere. Sorry."

"I think we need to park that side of it for the

minute and change tack. Does anybody know anything about religious murders?"

"Apart from the three dead nuns in our last case do you mean," says Roy.

"Of course I do Roy. Don't be so stupid."

Silence descends which answers her question. "Roy, get on the web and see what you can find out about religious killings. Jason, get on HOLMES and do a search for any similar murders. I'm off to see if we've had any phone calls from the religious community about our corpse."

Back in the office she picks up the phone to check for messages. She is interrupted by a knock at the door. Jason enters, his face haggard. He looks as if he hasn't eaten for days.

"I'm sorry to disturb you ma'am."

"Sit down. You're not disturbing me. What can I do for you?"

He sits for a minute, his face anguished. She gives him time. "It's this injury ma'am. The needlestick. I'm really worried. I can't think of anything else. I can't concentrate."

"I thought your initial bloods came back negative for HIV?"

They did but they've sent one off to the laboratory. I won't get that for a couple of days. They need to test for hepatitis in about two weeks."

"Would you like a few days off until you get the results?"

"I don't think so ma'am. I have too much time to think when I'm not at work. I just wanted you to know how I was feeling."

"Thanks. Are you eating? You look like you need a square meal."

"No ma'am."

"Come with me. We're off down the canteen for

the biggest plate of stodge we can get. Tell the rest of the team though and you won't be worrying about HIV any more."

She is heartened to see the glimmer of a smile pull up the corners of his mouth. It's amazing what a plate of hearty Scottish cooking can do for moral. Especially when the boss pays for it.

She eventually gets back to the phone and the messages. The only message is from a computer saying she is entitled to PPI. Fraudsters are a bit thick if they don't remove the police station numbers from their computer programmes. Maybe her friends in uniform would like to do something about it?

She is spending a quiet few minutes sitting beside the fan whilst updating HOLMES when Douglas turns up with his kids. They are Rory and Alice, aged eleven and seven respectively. They are delightful children and she loves spending time with them as much as with Douglas.

"Well hello. What a pleasant surprise. What brings you to Bell St."

"Do you want to come to Pizza Hut for your tea? Daddy said he would take us." Alice's eyes are sparkling and she is hopping from one foot to the other.

"Please Shona. We really want you to come. You could tell us all about your case." Rory is an unusual lad in that he wants to do Shona's job. He has his career path mapped out already.

"Pizza sounds lovely but I don't think I ought to be discussing dead bodies in Pizza Hut. I might put people off their dinner." Grins and giggles follow. She grabs her handbag and tells the team they can clock off. Pizza sounds much better than bloodless bodies and unidentifiable corpses.

6

The cleaner views the room with a practiced eye, taking in every aspect of the job at hand. Carefully placing the tools of his trade just inside the door, he is dressed in full protective clothing. This is not a job where you leave anything to chance. Not one to be enjoyed but endured.

The formidable jet of a well used power hose is directed towards the gelatinous substance which coats the concrete surfaces. Pink liquid swirls down the nearby drain removing all signs of the previous contents. Not content with the result, the jet is used once more. An added reassurance that there is nothing left. No sign of filth or dirt.

Putting the hose outside, the cleaner grasps the long wooden handle of a stiff bristled brush. A quick dip in a bleach filled bucket and then, using powerful muscles, he scrubs every inch of the room. Dip, scrub, repeat. Dip, scrub, repeat. The monotony soothes him, and he uses the time to think. His thoughts are clear, a sparkling vision of what is yet to come.

Having finished this task he sweeps the room with piercing green eyes. He is aware of every miniscule detail of each surface. He scrapes remnants from the floor using a brand new putty knife, cleans it on a pristine cloth. The cloth is folded, carefully placed in a zip seal bag.

Another brush, an aluminium handle this time. Dipped in Hydrogen peroxide. Rhythmically moved over every perfect slab of concrete. Slowly, not one millimetre missed. He takes his time, proud of his handiwork.

Once the brushes and buckets have joined the power hose outside, the drain is filled with drain unblocker. It is the attention to detail which makes him so good at his job. Satisfied in a job well done, he leaves the room. The doors and windows are left wide open to allow the sun to continue the work of disinfecting the room. It is ready.

7

Shona should know that a rare night out would be a precursor to an early morning call from the duty sergeant. She'd gone home with Douglas to help tuck the kids up and read them a story. Then the adults spent a couple of pleasant hours drinking Talisker and setting the world to rights. This homely scenario had populated her dreams, but the ringing of the phone rudely shatters it.

"McKenzie." She has a head like a pot as they say in Dundee. She's not entirely sure what it means but is happy to go with the flow. Her sore head is more due to lack of sleep than whisky-fuelled indulgence. Waking at 5 a.m. after a late night is not conducive to good health.

"There's been another suspicious death ma'am." Sergeant Baines sounds in fine fettle considering he's been up all night.

"Where?" she forces through a tongue cleaving to the roof of her mouth.

"On the steps of Kings in Perth Road."

"Kings? Isn't that a church? Is it another vicar?"

"It is a church but I'm not sure about the vicar part. The young bobby who called it in seemed a bit upset. I think it's his first dead body."

"I'm on my way."

She needs caffeine but it is too hot for coffee. She stops at a twenty four hour place on the way up the Perth Rd and grabs an iced coffee. Extra strong. The church building looks like it is getting some well needed TLC as it is surrounded by scaffolding. It has the appearance of a building site rather than a church. There is indeed a dead body adorning the steps leading up to the front entrance. Despite the fact that the sun is showing its head over the rooftops it is still too dark in the doorway for her to see what the corpse is wearing. Railings bar her way to the body. Nodding to the POLSA she approaches the two PC's, standing beside him, one of whom looks a bit rattled.

"I take it you found him?"

"Yes ma'am."

"How exactly did you find him? It must have been pitch black and he's behind locked gates."

"We heard a noise ma'am and thought it might have been burglars. The scaffolding means it's easy access. It was only a cat but our torches lit up the body."

"Has anyone been in to check if he was only injured? The poor man might need medical assistance."

"No ma'am. We couldn't find an entrance. It's pretty obvious he's dead though. Even the POLSA agrees on that one."

This is like pulling teeth. She has to ask for every little detail. You'd think a couple of coppers could be a bit more forthcoming. "What gave you that impression?"

"He looks like he's been mauled by a lion ma'am."

The closest you'll get to a lion in Dundee are the ones at Edinburgh zoo, so she has a sneaky feeling that they have another murder on their hands. She needs to get at that body, quick as.

"Morning ma'am." Peter is behind her as are Nina and Roy. "Abigail will be here in a minute. She's getting a taxi," says Nina.

"Good. I've not got Jason up. I think he needs

sleep more than we need him here."

"You've a good heart ma'am."

"Don't you lot think I'm going soft. You'll all have to work harder to make up for the fact we're one man down." She calls over to the POLSA. Is anyone from the church on their way to open up.

"Yes but the key holder lives in the boondocks so it could be quite some time before they get here."

"If the body's in there then either someone with a key did it or there's another way in. Come on Peter we'll go and have a look."

Walking down the narrow side street, which runs down the side of the church, shows them nothing. It is all high walls and gates locked up tight as a miser's wallet. The frontage has them no further forward with a similar array of railings and walls.

"Do you think they could have thrown the body over the railings?"

"Not unless they're Russian weight lifters. I'd say our dead body weighs about 18 stone give or take."

"Maybe it's the Alexyevs again."

"Please God no! Not again?" The Alexyev twins are a couple of Russian thugs who run some sort of racketeering business in the City. Shona's team have tried to charge them numerous times but they always seem to slip out of both handcuffs and charges as fast as an eel from a barrel. She's had a bellyful of them and their antics. "Looks like we're going to have to go over the wall."

"No' me. I'm far too old to be getting up tae antics like that. Plus I'll make a mess of my suit."

That would be a hard feat to undertake since his suit already looks like he hasn't taken it off in a month. Peter isn't famed for his sartorial style. "Fine. Send me Roy and Iain. We'll do it."

By a judicious amount of heaving and shoving they

are soon over the wall and approaching the body.

A mixture of early morning light and a torch soon shows them they have another dead vicar on their hands. Once again his chest is open to the world and a cross is etched deeply into the flesh.

"Looks like another serial killer, Ma'am," says Iain. He is far too cheerful about it for Shona's liking. Still, as Iain is their resident fingerprint and crime scene expert he probably thinks he's in seventh heaven. There's lots of lovely evidence to be found and collected.

"Let's not get ahead of ourselves. Two bodies does not a serial killer make."

"Don't bet on it, Ma'am. You seem to attract serial killers like a dog in heat."

"Roy. You might want to rephrase that. I hear Tesco are hiring when you need a new job."

"Sorry ma'am."

"Don't give me that crap. You're never sorry. Iain, get some photographs."

He responds by pulling a top of the range Canon from his bag. Police Scotland has found some money from somewhere and spent it upgrading technology. Iain thinks all his birthdays have come at once and Peter thinks he has gone straight to hell without passing go.

"Our corpse isn't as smelly as the last one. He looks a bit smarter as well," says Roy.

"I wouldn't quite have put it that way but you're right. He appears a tad more respectable."

Just as Iain is finishing the photos, the key holder arrives to unlock the gates.

"Thanks. Can you stay here we'll need to speak to you."

"Aye. I'll be over there." He points to the shade of a nearby shop canopy.

Before Shona can get near the body the Police Surgeon, Larry Briar, arrives with the Procurator Fiscal not far behind him. Larry goes to examine the deceased and Douglas stops beside her.

"Morning Shona."

"Have you dumped Rory and Alice with your poor mother again."

"My poor mother? She loves it. I thought as I was kid free I'd come and find out what's going on."

"Another dead vicar. Looks like he's as bloodless as the first."

"Why would anyone want to be killing vicars, never mind draining them of their blood? Is it some sort of satanic ritual?"

"That's about as good a guess as any. I was beginning to think that myself."

Larry hurries past, mopping his brow with a huge spotted hankie, saying, "Definitely dead, probably due to the cross decorating his chest."

"Thanks Larry," but she is speaking to his back, which is fleeing towards the air-conditioned comfort of his car. Shona feels like joining him.

Douglas and Shona go to examine the crime scene.

"That chap's a bit on the rotund side, and there appears to be very little disturbance around the area," says Larry.

"How on earth did they get him here?" replies Shona.

"Heaven only knows."

"That was dreadful Sir." Nina has joined them.

"I thought it was good considering it's only 6.30 am and I'm standing in a puddle of sweat."

"When everyone's quite finished creating a comedy scene could we get down to some business?"

"I'll leave you to it and stop distracting your team."

Shona walks Douglas to the gate to say goodbye to

him. As he leaves she hears Roy saying, “We're solving a murder and the DI's playing tonsil hockey with the Procurator Fiscal.”

“Don't be so damn well cheeky Roy.” Heat rises in her face.

“Aw, look at that. Are ye going all coy on us now ma'am,” says Peter.

“You lot, get on with your work and leave my love life out of this.”

“Well if you will conduct your romance with dead bodies at your feet what do you expect?”

“Shut up Nina. Back to work and the next person to mention my love life will be tapping the boards outside the dole office. Is that clear enough for you?” Thankfully most of them decide she's had enough and turn their attention elsewhere. Roy on the other hand.

“He'll be back soon enough ma'am. I'm sure you'll find another body to whisper sweet nothings over.”

“You obviously feel breathing is overrated Roy.”

“Why?”

“Because if you don't keep your mouth shut you won’t be in a position to breathe once I'm finished with you.”

He finally gets the message. The press, however, do not. Everything is conspiring to send her into a gleefully police free early retirement today. Despite the early morning there are a duo of reporters outside the gates.

“You lot are like fleas on a camel. Always buzzing around and you give me a rash.”

“Freedom—”

“I don't want to hear it. You can be as free as a bird outside my crime scene. Now run along.”

“Don’t be so condescending.”

“I'll condescend you right into a cell if you don't step back beyond the crime tape. You are severely testing my patience. I don't swear but I'm so close to it it's putting me in a bad mood. So buzz off."

They, like Roy, take the hint and disappear. Thank goodness, thinks Shona. This lack of food, due to supporting Peter with his diet, is giving her low blood sugar. She's not in the mood for arguing with fools.

Leaving them all to it Shona decides to have a word with the key holder, who turns out to be a Mr Zachariah Warrington. He is one of the elders of the church.

After showing him her badge Shona says, "Thanks for coming out so early. Are you happy to answer a few questions?"

"Of course, would you like to go inside the church? We can sit in the office?"

"We might need to search the building first. This won't take long. Who is the Vicar here?"

"Dennis Aldgate. He's been in post for about six years. He's on a three month sabbatical in Vietnam at the moment, doing missionary work."

It's a great life being a Vicar, thinks Shona. The furthest the firm has sent her is Aberdeen for a conference.

"Who would have keys to the church?"

"I do, as do three other elders, the church secretary, the cleaners and our outreach worker. The builders probably have one at the moment too. They need to get in and out to do interior work."

"Shona thinks that's an awful lot of people to be given free rein access to the church. "I'll need to speak to them all. I will also need to have a longer talk to you. Would you be able to come down to the station later?"

"Of course, what time would you like me? Can I go home and have a shower first?"

"That shouldn't be a problem. Please don't tell anyone about what you have seen. We will inform them when appropriate."

"See you later," and he leaves.

"Time for a search, boys and girls," she calls out to the team.

"It's been a long time since I was called a boy." Thankfully Peter is grinning. It occurs to Shona that she could get in bother for such sayings in today's PC culture. Sod it, she thinks. She knows her team well enough after a couple of years, to realise that she can get away with anything she says. Her disparate team has solidified and she has gained their respect.

"You get the gist. Spread out and search every inch. Anything you find is to be snagged, tagged, bagged and straight into evidence."

"It's a building site. There's rubbish everywhere."

"I appreciate that. Use your common sense. From the looks of our dead man I'd say he wasn't killed by a blow with a lump of concrete."

"There aren't many footprints ma'am. The grounds baked as hard as the concrete."

"For Pete's sake. Would you all stop saying what you can't do and get on with doing what you can do. You're Dundee's top team. Act like it."

"Can I do one more search for footprint impressions before we start. The newest ones are likely to be whoever brought our victim in here."

"Fill your boots."

"Ma'am that was awful," says Nina.

"It's the best you're going to get given this heat. My brain's frazzled. Hurry it up before we all die of heat exhaustion." Ambling over to her car Shona pulls out some bottles of water and distributes them. "Here, keep hydrated."

The team slug them down like the finest whisky.

"You're a life saver ma'am," says Roy.

"It'll be your life we'll need to save if you get sweat

all over my crime scene. I'm being realistic, not nice."

Sending one of the uniforms to get a supply of bottled water she gets into a full body suit. Iain, also fully suited, is almost finished the photographs.

"When you're done I'll tote the portable UV and we can look for body fluids," says Shona.

"That'll be fun given the weather. Every builder, and the whole population of the church will have been milling around in this garden."

"I know. It doesn't bear thinking about."

When she gets back to the gate there are several builders standing at the crime scene tape. A man, who is obviously their gaffer, is arguing with Peter."

"We're losing money here. If we don't finish on time we won't get paid."

"I know that, but your building site's now a crime scene. You cannae go in," says Peter.

"What am I meant to do wi' all my boys if they can't work."

Shona steps in. "You can send them all down to Bell Street station. We need to interview everyone, including you."

"We havnae done anything. We've not got time to be sitting around in a police station."

"The quicker you get there. The quicker you can get on with finding other work."

"My boss won't like this."

"I'm investigating a crime. Your boss's hurt feelings are the least of my worries. Now move before I arrest you and take you down to the station myself." She turns to Peter. "I'm taking Roy with me to interview this lot. You're in charge. I'll see you back at the station."

8

The builders take their own sweet time getting there. They probably came via a greasy spoon cafe to get a full Scottish Breakfast and several mugs of builders brew tea, thinks Shona. Not that she blames them. She doesn't know how they do their work in this heat. She feels almost sorry for them. They interview the gaffer first.

"Interview with Mr Kevin Stevens, commenced at 1007 hours, Detective Inspector Shona McKenzie and Detective Constable Roy MacGregor in attendance."

Preliminaries over she asks, "Mr Stevens how long have you, and your men, been working at the church?"

"Three months. We've a deadline tae finish in six months. My boss won't like this. He's going to be mad when he finds out we're no' there."

"We'll sort that out for you later. During your time there have you noticed anything unusual."

"Nothing, unless you meant the fact they're all trying to convert us."

Shona is sure that's not the case but leaves it be. Getting into a religious discussion isn't going to move the case forward. "What about your men? Do you know them all? Has anyone new joined you?"

We've all been together for a few years. Apart from young Billy that is. This is his first job but he's Hamish's son."

"Whose Hamish?"

"One of my best plasterers. Billy's learning the trade."

"Did anything look out of the ordinary to you this morning?"

"Apart from the fact the place was swarming with polis do you mean."

"Of course that's what I mean."

"Okay. No need tae get shirty. I never got a close enough look to find out."

"Please could you stay here and I will get someone to take you down there later to have a look."

"I need to talk to my boss. He might have other work for us."

"Give us his details and we'll let him know."

"George Brown."

"Ex Lord Provost Brown?" Shona knew it could only be a matter of time before Pa Broon crawled into the case.

"Aye."

"We'll let him know."

She breaks the news of George Brown's involvement to the Chief.

"DI McKenzie, why is it that every case you deal with involves rattling the Ex Lord provost?"

"Considering he's got his fingers in every single Dundee pie, Sir, I can't move without tripping over him."

"Don't get cheeky with me. You need to deal with the builders and then let them go."

"Sir, they're potential witnesses."

"Don't you think I know that Shona? I've been doing this longer than you. Ask them what you have to and let them go."

"Sorry Sir. I will do."

The Chief ignores her as usual. She leaves, thinking longingly of burying him in the foundations of a building site.

The team are back, hot, hungry and grumpy.

"I need food. The wife won't care if I have a bacon roll." Peter is sporting the miserable look.

"Yes she will. There's no way I'm going against Mrs Johnston's wishes. I value my life too much. Come on. If Doreen or Annie are on I'm sure they'll do us all a healthy full cooked. That should keep the wolf from the door until you eat your packed lunch."

"That's the ticket ma'am. Maybe this diet lark isn't as bad as I thought."

Shona is thinking it's a bit hot for a cooked breakfast, but if it keeps Peter in a good mood she is willing to make the sacrifice.

An interview room is featuring heavily in Shona's day. This time Nina accompanies her as she interviews Zachariah Warrington, the elder from Kings.

"Thank you for coming in Mr Warrington."

"Please call me Zach. We're all very friendly at Kings. No standing on ceremony."

"Zach. What can you tell me about your church."

"We're an evangelical congregation, a breakaway from the mainstream church."

"How big is your church."

"We have a couple of hundred regulars. Some more on our books who don't come often."

Keeping her face outwardly calm, Shona groans inwardly. That's a lot of people to interview if it comes down to it. She might as well take an ad out in *The Courier* and interview everyone at once.

"You say you're a breakaway church. Was there any animosity?"

"We broke away over a point of doctrine. It was all fairly amicable."

Shona pushes over a photo of the dead vicar. "Do

you recognise this man."

Zach studies it for a minute. "He looks vaguely familiar. I can't place him though. I meet a lot of people through the church and in my job."

"What is your job?"

"I work for an oil company. I commute to and from Aberdeen."

"Can anyone vouch for your whereabouts last night?"

"I was at home with my wife and family. It was my twin sons' thirtieth birthday. We had a party."

"After we've taken your fingerprints you're free to go. Could you email through a list of contact details for anyone who holds a key?" She hands him a business card with her details. Since Police Scotland decided that the job was all about community engagement they'd been issued with corporate cards. Shona is unimpressed, as the place still seems to be crawling with crazies no matter how much money they spend on business cards.

Going back to the squad room she bangs into Jason who is looking his usual bright and cheerful self.

"You've obviously had good news Jason."

"The best news. All my blood results came back negative. It looks like I'm in the clear."

"I'm glad to hear it. We'll have a celebratory drink later."

The team is in a jubilant mood when they hear the news.

"So you didn't need that laze in your pit this morning after all, Soldier Boy," says Roy.

"I agree. While the rest of us were working you were tucked up wi' your teddy bear," adds Peter.

Jason, grinning ear to ear, says, "The first drinks are on me tonight to make up for it."

"Now you're talking." Nina is never one to turn down a free drink.

"Hold off on the celebrations you lot. Remember we've a couple of dead vicars on our hands. Jason, you can come with me. We're off to the Gateway to see if they know our new victim."

"Slow down ma'am, you're a bit fast," says Jason.

"For an ex soldier you're a right wuss. My driving's fine."

"With all due respect ma'am, I've seen tank drivers in battle who drive better than you."

"Don't be cheeky. Shut your eyes you big baby."

Silence falls. In Jason's case it is accompanied by white knuckles and clutching of the door handle. You just can't get the cops these days, thinks Shona. Act like a cowardly wee baby the minute any danger arrives.

They manage to get to the Gateway without a mishap. Jason is out of the door and on his feet before she can fully pull the handbrake.

"Can I take the wheel on the way back to the station?"

"Honestly Jason, how can you be such a coward? If it makes you feel better then yes. I do want to get back there today though."

Candace Sanchez is in, and as Peter had alluded to, exudes Southern hospitality. "Can I get you a cold soda?" she asks.

Shona asks for a diet coke and Jason for an Irn Bru. When Candace goes to fetch them Shona says, "Hoy. We're meant to be supporting Peter on his diet."

"Och, Ma'am. Peter isn't here and after everything I've been through I deserve fully loaded."

"Are you going to bring up your needlestick injury for the rest of time?"

"I'm talking about my trip in the car with you, not my close shave with HIV."

The return of Candace stops her from adding him to the body pile. Shona pushes over the photo of their latest victim. "Do you know this man?"

"I can't say I do. Would you like me to ask some of my congregation?"

"Thanks. Could you let us know if you have any joy?" Shona hands out another business card. They at least save the hassle of writing numbers down.

"Of course Ma'am, I'm always happy to help law enforcement."

The drive back to the police station is uneventful, if a little slow for Shona's taste.

Back in Bell Street there seems to be bodies everywhere. Shona can barely get to the squad room.

"What's going on? Why is half the population of Dundee cluttering up my station?"

"They're from the church and the builders. We're interviewing them and taking fingerprints," says Roy.

"Did no one think to stagger the times? There are more people here than at a Tannadice home game."

"For someone who disnae like football you don't half talk about it a lot."

"Peter, you're heading for a job in Traffic. Is Iain doing all the fingerprinting on his own?"

"He is. The rest of us are interviewing."

"I don't see much evidence of interviewing. You're all loafing around in here."

"Relax, Ma'am. We're just having a tea break. We've done ten already," says Nina.

"Fair enough. You'd better give that lot bottles of water or they're going to be screaming police torture. A trek through the Sahara dessert would be cooler than this place."

"Right you are. Come on you lot. Let's keep the natives happy."

"Not so fast. Roy, I want you to go through missing persons. Cover the whole of Scotland. Jason, go and help Iain with the fingerprinting. The rest of us can split up and do the interviews."

Three hours later they are no further forwards on the investigation but seem to be short of a couple of builders.

"Get hold of the gaffer and ask where his workers are. Tell him we'll arrest him if he doesn't bring them in looking meek and mild."

"Arrest him for what, Ma'am?" asks Abigail.

"For annoying me. Of course we won't arrest him, but he doesn't know that."

"They're probably illegal immigrants. They'll have disappeared into the wind." Abigail isn't giving up her point of view, without a fight.

"I'm sure you're right but turn the thumbscrews on Kevin anyway. He might cough them up."

"You're affy optimistic for someone with your track record, if you don't mind me saying."

"Peter, you can always be relied on to state the obvious." Her grin softens her words.

They turn the thumbscrews on Kevin, with a couple of other torture procedures thrown in for good measure. He still can't help them with their enquiries.

"They were Romanian. They're probably back there now."

"Where in Romania?"

"How the fu..."

The sound of Shona's hand slamming on to the table reverberates round the room.

"Keep it clean in my nick. I take it you brought the

paperwork we asked for."

"No. I dinnae know where it is. You're the police. Find them yourself."

"Peter, chuck this waste of oxygen into a cell."

"What for? I've not done anything wrong. You can't arrest me."

"I'm arresting you under the Immigration, Asylum and Nationality Act 2006 for employing illegal immigrants."

"They were European. They're allowed to work here."

"Not from Romania. They need a permit. We'll let you phone whoever you need to get the relevant paperwork and permit brought here."

"I want a lawyer."

"I thought you might. Peter, let him ring his lawyer."

Once Kevin the Gaffer is comfortably ensconced in a cell, Peter joins Shona in her office.

"Ma'am, you do know we can't keep him in a cell for employing illegal immigrants. He's no' exactly a danger to society."

"He's a flight risk."

Peter looks askance at her.

"Okay. I know. The likelihood of him fleeing his beloved Dundee is zero. Keep him a couple of hours and then throw him out. He's waiting for his lawyer anyway."

"Do you enjoy terrorizing the good citizens of Dundee?"

"Love it. It's my favourite pastime."

"Ma'am, you've brought something special to the job."

"I aim to please. Now go and see if you can find the wayward Romanians."

Shona leaves it a couple of hours before wandering in to the main office.

"Still no Romanians then Peter?"

Unless you want me to buy a ticket to Eastern Europe then I think we're fresh out of luck on that one."

"What about our dead vicars? Do they fit the description of any missing persons?"

"We've a few likely hits ma'am," says Roy. "They're a bit spread out though."

"Where exactly?"

"The Shetlands, Dumfries and Galloway, Fife, Orkney, and the Outer Hebrides."

"Send the local bobbies photos. Ask them if they'll speak to the relatives. You and I can go to Fife. Grab the details." The thought of an air conditioned car propels Roy from the room.

9

St Andrews is parading its magnificent, ancient splendour, sunlight highlighting the medieval stones of the 14th Century university buildings. A myriad of narrow lanes and streets leads them to a brightly painted front door that doesn't look big enough to allow an adult to enter. It is opened by a woman dressed in tailored shorts, every hair on her head perfectly placed. When the woman speaks, Shona forms the opinion that the hairs are probably terrified to move.

"What do you want? I'm busy. I'm not buying anything."

Shona's seamlessly placed foot and the flash of an ID card stops the door in its tracks.

"DI McKenzie and DC MacGregor. We need to talk to you."

The door opens again and the women ushers them in with an imperious sweep of her arm.

"Mrs Farraday, we are here about your husband."

These words are usually a cue for a white face and clutching of chest. This woman's face doesn't even twitch.

"Why do you need to know about him now? He's been missing for years."

"We've found a body that looks like your husband. We would like you to take a look at a photo?"

"I doubt it's him. I'm sure he went off with someone who had more money than me. That's all he was interested in."

Shona shows her the photo.

"It does look a bit like him. I doubt he'd look like that now though. He's 15 years older."

"Can you tell us what dentist he used?"

"Phillips in Canongate."

"Thank you Mrs Farraday. We'll be in touch."

They return to the fold via Phillips the Dentist who says he will send the records through to them.

"Can we get a McDonalds on the way back?" asks Roy.

"Not on your nelly. We're diet city remember."

"But I don't need to be on a diet. Peter won't know."

"The amount of crap you eat you'll need to be on one soon. Better to take preventative action. Peter will smell junk food off your breath at a million paces, as you well know."

Roy looks belligerent but wisely drops the matter. The ride home is quiet.

Peter hasn't managed to dig up the Romanians. Shona decides to give up the search. "It's a waste of manpower. They'll never be back in the UK. The likelihood of them being our murderer is less than zero," she says.

The Chief is on the warpath and looking for her. "Why are you traipsing round the countryside whilst George Brown's Building Manager is languishing in one of my cells?"

"He was employing illegal immigrants Sir."

"Whilst you can charge him with that, he doesn't need to be in a cell. Release him."

"Yes sir."

"You can ring George Brown and apologise to him as well. I'm fed up of him complaining about you and your antics."

"Apologise to Pa Broon? Sir—"

"Don't even think about disobeying me. Do it now. Is that clear?"

"Of course Sir." She thought about tying the Chief and Pa Broon together and dumping them in the Tay Estuary.

Going to release the builder, Shona finds a disgruntled Angus Runcie.

"Why have you arrested my client? This is preposterous. How dare you. This is police persecution."

Angus is a solicitor who Shona is convinced is dodgier than his clients. He also seems to be at George Brown's beck and call.

"You're in luck. I'm just about to release your client. Your bank balance will be glad to know he's been charged under Immigration, Asylum and Nationality Act 2006 for employing illegal immigrants."

"You cannot keep him in a cell for that."

"I was making enquiries and wanted to make sure he was comfortable whilst he waited."

"In a jail cell?"

"Why are we still arguing the toss about this. He's free to go which means you can take him with you."

"You haven't heard the end of this."

"I'm sure I haven't. Have a nice day now." She turns and walks out of the room. It's at times like this she loves her job.

The day continues to be frustrating with nothing to move the case forward. Shona gives Double Eckie a ring. It had taken her a while to realise this was Scottish slang for Alexander Alexander. As well as having a name you needed a translator to understand, he is also the facial profiler for the unit. He is so old, Shona thinks he was there at the inception of Tayside Police. However, he is the most brilliant profiler in history and no one wants to retire him. This despite the fact there are much more modern methods. When Eckie shuffles off this mortal coil they'll replace him with a slick youngster wielding a computer programme rather than a pencil.

"I take it you've a dead body you need me to draw, Shona?"

"I have. Could you come up?"

"Put the kettle on."

By the time Double Eckie arrives Shona has a cup of builders brew tea and a couple of chocolate biscuits ready for him. The diet can only go so far.

Even the Chief agrees that the profile pictures are worthy of an award.

"I'll be sad to see Mr Alexander go when he retires." Formality is alive and well and living in the Chief's office thinks Shona.

"I'm sure we all will Sir. I will get it sent to D.C. Thomsons now. I'm sure it will be front page news in *The Courier* in the morning."

The Chief is ignoring her as per.

The team are hard at work when Shona returns to the office. Apart from Peter that is. He is keeping himself busy with a copy of *The Dundee Evening Telegraph*, a mug of tea and a KitKat biscuit, which is halfway to his lips.

"Peter. Put that biscuit down at once. Your wife will have a fit."

"Ma'am. I need something to keep body and soul together. It's been a hard day."

"Yeah. Right. You're reading the paper, that's not

exactly hard work. I've strict instructions from Mrs Johnston to keep you on the straight and narrow."

"You mean the wife's got you spying on me?"

"Of course she has. She's been married to you for thirty years. She knows exactly what you're like."

Abigail interrupts, preventing Peter's total meltdown.

"Who fancies going for a slap up authentic Chinese meal?" she asks. "I've got my mother and four sisters here and we'd like you to join us."

"Four sisters? I thought the Chinese only had one kid. How come there's so many in your family?"

"Roy, you're as thick as a mountain climbing haggis, only more rare. I'm from the Isle of Skye, not Beijing."

"I wasn't trying to be racist. I was just wondering."

"Roy you're safe. Chill. Now are you coming for this Chinese or not?"

His coat is on and he is out the door so fast that Abigail can't keep up. Shona guesses that the woman has a date. Not much of a date though as most of the team follow just as quickly. Also Shona wouldn't foist Roy on the poor woman. She quite likes her.

Stopping only to say to Peter, "You'd better ring the wife and invite her as well. She can tell you what you can eat," she flees from the room.

Peter's grin signifies all is well in his world.

10

When Shona arrives at the Gulags the next day, she opens an email from the dentist. Attached is a beautifully clear set of pristine photos. The missing Mr Farraday has arrived in the station, or his teeth have anyway. Shona picks up the phone to ring Mary, the pathologist for Dundee.

"Shona. You're up to your usual tricks I see. I knew it would only be a matter of time before we spoke again."

Shona has given up trying to defend her reputation as Dundee's answer to the grim reaper. She has decided to embrace it and wear it as a badge of honour.

"You know me. I like to keep things lively."

"You certainly do. Decorated corpses are a new high even for you."

"I've emailed you some dental records. Can you check and see if they fit our new corpse?"

"Is later today okay? I'll give you a ring. One bit of news. Your first corpse was embalmed."

"Embalmed? Why would anyone want to embalm someone and then dump them?"

"Thankfully it's your job to find out. I only look after them with the utmost care whilst they are under my roof. Your job wouldn't be my cup of peppermint tea at all."

"I'm not thinking much of it either at the moment. Speak soon."

Hanging up, she grabs a double strength Brazillian blend coffee and heads back to her desk. The local papers beckon.

‘Do You Know these Men?

‘Dundee Clergy in a Murderer’s Grip.’

‘Dundee CID investigates the deaths of two unidentified men. Sources close to the investigation say the men were killed in the most horrific way. Could another serial killer be holding Dundee in their murderous vice?’

The article continues in the same vein for several paragraphs. Not that Shona is surprised. The local press seem to think that persecuting her is written into their job descriptions. At least the photographs are nice and clear. That will surely bring someone forward to identify the victims she thinks. For once the press might just help them. What was the saying about wonders and ceasing she thinks.

By the time she's finished both the papers and the coffee the others have arrived.

“Embalmed?” says Peter. “You did say embalmed?”

“I most certainly did.”

“From dead nuns to embalmed vicars. Only you could manage that little trick Ma'am,” says Nina.

“Everyone's a critic. Never mind blaming me. What are we going to do to find our murderer cum embalmer?”

“If we're talking embalming then maybe we should look at the undertakers,” says Peter.

“And there are how many undertakers in Dundee?” asks Shona.

“I'll get on to yell dot com and find out,” says Roy.

“Not so fast flash Harry,” says Peter. “Use the paper version as well.”

Roy's raised brows shows he doesn't think much of that idea.

"Why would we do that?"

"To make sure we've got them all. Not everything's on your bl... blasted computer. Anyhow we should start with Slick Andra."

"Does nobody have a normal name in Dundee? Who's Andra, slick or otherwise?" asks Shona.

"The street name for Andrew Claypotts, of Claypotts, Ratray and Elgin, funeral directors to the Dundee underworld."

"Have I been teleported to New York? Why would the criminal fraternity of Dundee have their own undertaker?"

"If you're going to bump them off you might as well make a bit of money out of it."

"Roy. That's low even for you. It's not funny."

"For once he's no' being funny. It's true."

Shona blinks then says, "Bring him in."

Slick Andra does indeed look slick. He is all brylcreemed hair and false obsequiousness. The creases in his black suit are so sharp they are likely to cut him. Smarmy little git is Shona's first thought.

"How can I help you fine officers of the law? Have you got a body which needs my specialist skills?"

"We'd like you to come to an interview room. We need to ask you a few questions?"

"What about? I run a respectable business."

"Then you've nothing to fear."

The preliminaries over, Shona shoves the photos of the two dead men across the table. "Have you seen either of these men before?"

A quick glance. "I meet a lot of people in my job. I can't remember them all."

"You might want to look a bit more closely at these ones."

"I've already told you I don't know them."

"Mr Claypotts, if you don't look at these photos properly then you're going to find yourself in one of your own coffins. I'm fast losing patience with you."

"No need to get shirty." He studies the photos. "No. I have never seen them in my life before."

"They could be clergymen."

"I meet many people of the cloth in my line of work. I can assure you officer that I have never met these particular men." There was that obsequious smile again. Shona has a sudden urge to wipe it off his face permanently.

"Where were you on the nights of April 13th and 14th?"

"How am I supposed to know? I don't have my diary with me?"

"Are you telling me a man such as yourself wouldn't have an electronic diary."

"My secretary keeps my diary."

"The DI's talking about the middle o' the night Andra. Stop playing games. We've no' got time for this."

His hand reaches into the inside of his freshly pressed jacket and pulls out an iPhone 6 plus. Shona thinks the funeral business must pay well.

"I was at home both nights."

"Why on earth didn't you say that in the first place? Can anyone vouch for that?" asks Shona.

"Yes, my husband can. We recently adopted a baby from China so we don't go out much."

"Thank you Mr Claypotts. We will be in touch with him. You are free to go."

"I never knew Andra was that way inclined," says Peter. "I'm sure his dad's no' very pleased. He's a bit o' a bampot. The dad that is. Although I'm sure Andra's just as bad."

"Stop whittering Peter. I don't care what way he's inclined. That's none of our business. However, his business is our business."

"Could you make that statement a bit more confusing, Ma'am. It wisnae quite baffling enough."

Laughing Shona says, "We're going to be crawling all over Claypotts, Ratray and Elgin. His smile gives me the impression he's right up to the armpits of his expensive black wool suit in crap."

"I'm no' a violent man, Ma'am, but even I felt like giving him a slap or two."

"I'll admit he gives me the creeps but you can't go around slapping witnesses."

"Of course not. It doesn't stop me thinking it would be a good idea though."

"Keep it like that."

Roy is busy looking at Facebook when Shona returns to the office.

"PC MacGregor, we're in the middle of a murder enquiry. What gives you the impression it would be a good idea to catch up on your social life?"

"I'm on the Scottish Police site seeing if anyone else has missing men."

"Roy, even a meathead like you knows that you'd be better off on HOLMES. Shut it down. I've a job for you."

"Anything interesting Ma'am?"

"Look into the goings on of our Andra's funeral parlour."

"That sound's deadly boring, Ma'am"

"Seriously Roy. If you enter the Police Christmas Review I'm bringing tomatoes with me."

She can hear his laugh all the way back to her office.

Less than an hour later Roy is knocking at the door.

"I've got some good news and some bad news, Ma'am."

"Spit it out. I want to move this investigation forward. At the moment it's as dead as the vicars."

"The good news is I've dug up a fair old bit about Andra and his good and not so good deeds."

"Come on Roy. Get to the point. I've enough suspense without you building it."

"It looks like the Alexeyevs are part owners of Andra Claypotts's family business."

"I hope you're joking."

"Nope. Gen up."

Shona slumps in her chair. The Russian twins again are all she needs.

The Chief refuses to allow her to interview the Alexeyevs.

"There is absolutely nothing linking them to this investigation, Shona. Find more proof."

"Sir—"

"Don't even bother arguing with me. Do what you're told for once. Now go and investigate without involving the Alexeyevs." Then he adds, "Or George Brown."

Shona leaves, wondering how she could have him put in one of Andra's caskets and buried alive.

This, the heat, and a lack of suspects or witnesses is putting her in a bad mood. She glowers at Abigail who takes it in her stride.

"Someone's come forward to say that he might have some information."

"Put him in an interview room. You can come with me."

It turns out the witness doesn't know the dead men. However, he has the name of someone he saw coming out from the Gateway gardens on the night of the 13th April at midnight, one Mr Charlie Souter. He had known him from school and was convinced it was him.

"Do you know where he lives?"

"The Cleppie Road somewhere, last I heard."

"Where?"

"Clepington Road. Do you no' speak English."

Shona has to stop her hands from squeezing his throat.

Roy and Jason bring Charlie in.

"He's not quite right in the head."

"Roy, what have I told you about treating people equally? You've still got to go on that course you know."

"Ma'am. He's right," says Jason.

Shona's brows arch so high they could double as the McDonald's sign. "Did I just hear right? You pair are agreeing?"

"We are Ma'am. You'll find out soon enough."

"Interview with Mr Charles Souter. DI Shona McKenzie and DS Peter Johnston in attendance."

"You cannae call me that."

"Call you what?" asks Shona.

"Charles."

"Why not?"

"Because it's no' my name."

"What is your name?"

"Charlie Soutar."

"Is that the name on your birth certificate?"

"No."

"So what is?"

"Charles Soutar."

"What? You just said your name isn't Charles."

"It isnae. Everybody calls me Charlie. I've always

been Charlie."

Shona and Peter exchange looks. This is going to be painful.

"Okay Charlie. Is it all right for me to call you Charlie?"

"I've just said. It's my name."

Shona sighs. The boys were right.

"Charlie, can you tell me where you were at midnight on April 13th?"

"When?"

"The 13th of April at midnight. What were you doing?"

A long silence follows. Peter can't bear it any longer.

"I should be at home spending quality time harassing my family not having cosy chats wi' you. Hurry up and talk. I'm growing bored here."

"I'm thinking. Give me time."

"I've seen sloths that move faster than your thinking process. I didnae have a beard when we came in here."

"Sergeant Johnston stop picking on the poor man. He'll think quicker without you jumping down his throat."

"Poor man…"

Shona grins. It's not often that Peter is short of a smart remark.

"I am beginning to agree the sergeant has a point though. We only asked you what you were doing on Thursday night, not the square root of Pi."

"What are you talking about? You're confusing me."

Shona takes a deep breath. "What were you doing on Thursday at 12 o'clock at night? I can't put it any more plainly than that." Even Shona wishes he'd hurry up and answer. The likelihood of him having committed their murder is zero, as he is as thick as a mealy pudding. They still have to go through the motions though.

"I went to my mums for tea. I always go there for tea on a Thursday. We have mince and tatties."

Shona can see Peter slumping further in his chair.

"At midnight?"

"After that we watch the telly. She's got Sky so she lets me watch the football."

"What's your mum's number so we can check that out?" The number exchanged, Peter goes to do the necessary check. Shona asks a passing PC to find a cup of tea for their witness and stay with him until she returns.

Ten minutes later she has her answer. The alibi checks out. Another dead end.

"Who was our mysterious man leaving the Gateway then? Get on to Holmes and see if anyone matching Charlie's description is known to us."

"I'm glad he checked out. I don't think I could bear the thought of having that poor soul in a cell. I don't think he'd know what to do," says Peter.

"You're right. Persecuting the vulnerable is not one of my favourite occupations."

Little does she know things are about to take an interesting turn.

11

Shona is sitting thinking in her office and drinking freshly brewed light cinnamon roast coffee. Nina barges through the door and batters into Shona's desk. Shona jumps up as coffee slops out of the mug. Grabbing tissues they both mop it up.

"For Pete's sake Nina. Can't you knock and come in quietly like a normal person?"

"Sorry, Ma'am." Her face says otherwise. "We've found someone on HOLMES who looks like our midnight visitor. He's known to us."

"Details?"

"Shawn Ratray. Aged 25. Lives in Fintry."

"Ratray? Is he related to the funeral directors?" Shona is catching Nina's excitement.

"Not a clue, but given the fact most people in Dundee seem to be related in some way then I'd say so."

"Go and bring him in."

"He was arrested for possession of an offensive weapon last time. He might not come quietly."

"You and I can go, along with Peter and Jason."

"Jason? He'll come back injured. You like to live life on the edge don't you?"

"He needs to learn to get out of the way. Anyway this will make up for his little lie in the other day."

"Are you going to hold that against him for the rest of his career?"

"Yep. It will come up in his final leaving speech."

Stab vests on, and weapons at the ready they present themselves at the front door of Shawn Ratray's house. They listen to the chimes of a doorbell echo through the flat.

"It sounds empty to me," says Jason.

"It does. Rattle the letterbox just to make sure," says Shona.

Jason gives it a vigorous rattle.

"Okay soldier boy. Keep the door in the frame."

The door opens, and then stops suddenly on a chain. A man dressed in nothing but a pair of boxer shorts and a drooping fag stands behind it. He bears more than a passing resemblance to Charlie Soutar. Replace Charlie's vacant look with a snarl and a pugilists nose, and they could be twins. Shona thinks they're probably related. Who the heck knows who's related to whom in all of this? Shawn takes one look at them and attempts to slam the door shut. It is stopped by Shona's foot and the full weight of Peter and Jason hurling themselves at the door. It shakes on its hinges and the man runs. Another concerted effort and the door gives way.

"Watch out, he could have a gun," Shona shouts.

They enter the flat, pistols at the ready. Jason was right. It is empty. No carpets, a couple of chairs and a mattress seem to be it. They advance slowly. They can't hear a sound. Then, seeing a movement Shona turns. The others follow a microsecond behind. Shawn's tattooed hands are clutching a solid plank of wood. It is complete with a nasty looking nail, a weapon meant to inflict maximum damage.

"Put it down Shawn."

"Fu—"

"Put it down. It will be better for you if you do."

Shawn roars and swings the weapon at Jason, who ducks. A crack echoes through the apartment. The sound of the wood hitting Peter's skull.

Shawn stumbles and Nina and Jason take the chance to grab him. Shawn finds himself with a mouthful of gun muzzle.

“Don't even think of twitching a muscle. I have an urge to shoot you which is so strong I am having trouble suppressing it,” says Shona.

Once Shawn is handcuffed Shona says, “Take him to the car and get him buckled in. Phone an ambulance. I'll go with Peter to the hospital.”

Shawn is dragged off, each step accompanied by obscenities. Shona can hear Nina saying, “Shut up or I’ll put gaffer tape over your mouth.”

The din recedes and Shona turns back to Peter who is sitting on the ground. The linen hankie he has pressed to his head is now a bright shade of red.

“I'm fine Shona. I dinnae need an ambulance.”

“Your getting one and that's an order. There's a lot of blood. I don't think it was the nail that hit you though. Thank God and I mean that literally.”

A couple of hours later she is back at the salt mines. She’s left Peter tucked up in a bed for an overnight stay, despite his protestations of “I dinnae need a fuss.” Mrs Johnston had arrived to relieve Shona of her babysitting duties. As Shona left, Mrs Johnston was busy telling Peter that no he couldn’t have a pudding for his tea. His injuries weren’t bad enough to warrant his straying from the path of dietary health. Shona decided that was a battle she didn’t want to be involved in.

On her return, Shawn Ratray isn’t any quieter. His bellows from the cells can be heard in every far-flung room in the station.

“Can we put some valium in his tea or something, Ma’am?” asks Roy.

“Much as I would love to rubber stamp your

request. We'd better not. Escort Mr. Ratray to a cell. You can join me in interr… er interviewing him."

"I'm no talking to any effing woman. You should be chained to a cooker."

"Listen here sunshine. Say that again and you'll need a straw to drink your meals. You'll talk to me and like it."

"No I fu…"

"PC MacGregor. Can you go and get that truncheon Sergeant Johnston keeps in his desk. It looks like we may be needing it."

"Righty ho, Ma'am"

"I want my lawyer."

"Does he happen to be Angus Runcie by any chance?"

His lawyer is indeed Angus Runcie. As well as being a lawyer he is also up to his fat neck in the various goings on of Dundee's underworld. He always seems to feature heavily in Shona's investigations. If Shona had her way he'd be conducting his business from a jail cell. The only person worse than him is his sister, Margaret McCluskey. The siblings are the bane of Shona's existence.

"You threatened my client. This is outrageous."

"I did no such thing. PC MacGregor did you hear me say I would lay a finger on Mr Ratray?"

"No, Ma'am."

"You threated to hit him with a truncheon."

"You'll find I didn't."

"I want to look at the recording of the interview."

"Be my guest. After our interview you are at liberty to view every recording we have. Now let's get a move on."

Shona strides off leaving Angus trailing in her

wake.

“Mr Ratray where were you on the night of April 13th?”

“Making out like a rabbit wi’ my latest whore. Where do you think I was?”

“Keep a clean mouth when you’re talking to me.”

“Fu…”

“Shona leans in close and her voice low says, “I’ve had enough of you. Unless you want to pay a final visit to the family funeral parlour then I suggest you answer my questions, and make it quick.”

“I told you. With a whore.”

“Does this particular whore have a name?”

“Delilah.”

“Any other details?”

“How would I know? I was sleeping with her, no’ proposing marriage.”

“I have a witness who says he saw you coming out of The Gateway gardens at midnight on that night.”

“I’m telling you I wisnae there.”

“My client is saying he was at home. Unless you produce this mysterious witness I am taking him home.”

“No so fast Angus. Your client has been arrested for battering my Sergeant with a lump of wood. He’s staying in my cells until I say otherwise. In the meantime I’ll be arranging an identity parade.”

The crash of a chair accompanies Ratray's change of position from sitting to standing. Shona's chair joins the melee as she steps back from being on the wrong end of a beating. Roy grabs the undertaker and Shona helps to cuff him.

“PC MacGregor escort Mr Ratray back to the cells.”

This is the cue for another bout of foul mouthed bellowing.

The table rattles as she bangs it with her fist. "Shut up. One more word from you and I'm adding disturbing the peace to your growing list of crimes."

She walks back to the office accompanied by the sound of blissful silence.

"Time to knock off chaps and chapesses. I've had a bellyful of Claypotts and Ratrys for the day. See you all bright and breezy for another thrilling instalment in the saga of Dundee CID."

Shona points her car in the direction of Monifieth. She thinks a visit to Douglas and the kids is in order. It will be nice to see Douglas without a dead body cluttering the place up.

12

The next morning finds six sweat soaked members of Dundee CID scurrying around the City. They are picking up volunteers for the identity parade. Peter is still lounging around in his pyjamas in a hospital ward.

"Why aren't we using VIPER?" asks Jason. VIPER is the acronym for Virtual Identity Parade, which is often used in modern day policing. Piloted in Scotland it's the preferred way of doing parades.

"Because I like persecuting the team. For goodness sake Jason, I want real live participants in a row. Our witness isn't exactly Einstein. Anything electronic might confuse him. I don't want him picking someone from the Outer Hebrides."

"Our suspect might be from the Outer Hebrides."

"I'm sure in the grey matter between your ears they could be. If you did more work and less griping the parade could be over and done with."

Their return to the station finds them with twelve willing volunteers for the lineup. However, there's one slight problem.

"I can't find the witness."

"Sorry Iain? I could swear you said you can't find the witness."

"I did. He gave us a false address."

"Let's hope he gave his real name. There can't be many Alexander Banaszewski's in Dundee. For goodness sake use your common sense and look up the electoral register."

Shona grabs one of the cream cakes she sneaked in, taking advantage of Peter's absence. Nina and Abigail are there before her.

"What's up with these youngsters? They're as thick as a haggis supper. Iain can find and use a spot of blood the size of a micron, ask him to think about finding a witness and he's clueless."

"In all fairness to the poor boy, Ma'am, he's used to puddling about in chemicals and disclosing solutions. I'm sure the nuances of Dundee geography have passed him by," says Abigail.

"I've sent him off to look at the electoral register. Surely it's not too much to ask that he could come up with that on his own. Go and give the twelve stooges a cup of tea. We'd better keep them sweet or their glowering looks will make them all look guilty."

"Shall we give them a cake each as well?" asks Nina.

"No you flaming well won't. Those cakes are all spoken for. We're not running a café."

Nina's dazzling smile would toast teacakes. "I was hoping you would say that."

Seventy minutes later they have their witness in an interview room.

"Why, exactly, did you lie to us about your address?" asks Shona.

"I was scared. I didn't want to get caught up in anything."

"Lying to the police means you could get caught up in a lot more than you wanted. Giving false information to the police is against the law in Scotland."

"I'm sorry. I was just trying to keep myself safe. I've seen them films. Criminals come after you. It's not good."

"For heavens sake, Mr Banaszewski. This is

Dundee not Chicago. Who on earth do you think is going to come after you? We're wasting more time. Come with me."

Shona stands the witness in front of one-way glass. Shuffling, he wipes his hands on his trousers.

"Mr Banaszewski you need to look through the window. No one inside can see you."

He pulls his gaze forward but a tell tale twitch appears under his eye. Shona turns to Nina, and says under her breath, "Get the lineup started before he collapses."

Minutes later the witness has identified Shawn Ratray. Shawn does not take it well and throws a punch at the pseudo suspect next to him. It lands square on his jaw and the man collapses. A couple of waiting cops join the brawl and yank Shawn Ratray to his feet. Alexander Banaszewski takes one look and bolts up the corridor with Shona in hot pursuit.

"Nina, get some medical attention for the injured stand in," she hollers over her shoulder.

Shona has broken the news to the Chief. He looks resigned.

"Shona, one of these days you will manage to carry out your duties without mayhem ensuing. You and your team are more like the Keystone Cops than a supposedly crack CID team. How you ever solve your cases is a mystery to me, but somehow you do. Try to keep everyone in one piece from now on."

Shona lleaves without thinking of ways to bump him off. Considering what had just happened she'd gotten off lightly.

Back in the interview room Shona is facing Shawn Ratray and is feeling much less magnanimous.

"You are in serious trouble. That's two counts of

assault to severe injury now. You are also beginning to piss me off. Unfortunately that's not an offence, but it doesn't bode well for your future. You'd better start talking."

"You can't talk to my client like that."

"Like what? I haven't said anything yet. Can we get on with the interview or are you thinking of challenging me every time I open my mouth?"

Angus snaps his mouth shut but his face lets Shona know she is dangerously close to a complaint. She couldn't care less. Angus Runcie is the least of her worries she thinks.

"Mr Ratray, it looks like your accounts of cavorting with a whore on the 13th April were greatly exaggerated. A witness has identified you as being at the Gateway."

"Who is it? I'll fu…"

Shona's raised voice is full of ice and crystal clear. "Mr Ratray, you do not want to issue threats in this room. Now were you at the Gateway?"

Silence, then, "Okay, I was, but only to see if there was anything worth nicking. I was trying to break in round the back."

"And you expect me to believe you?"

"It's the truth."

"You don't know the meaning of the word."

Shona hands him the identikit photos of the two men. "Do you know these men?"

"Apart from the fact they were plastered all over the front of the *Tele* do you mean?"

"Of course that's what I mean."

"Never seen them in my life."

"Well as one of them was found dead on the steps of the Gateway the same night you were there, forgive me if I don't believe you. I'm detaining you on suspicion of committing murder."

There is another fracas when Shawn makes a dive for Shona. Roy and Jason tackle him and they all descend in a heap on the floor. Angus Runcie leaps out of the way, trips, and lands facedown in the corner. In their last case a client who wasn't happy with Shona had thumped him. He'd obviously learnt that it was best to keep out of the way. Might be better to do it without falling though, thinks Shona.

Shona continues, "As I was saying. We are detaining you on suspicion of the murder of two unknown men. Shawn, this would be a good time to tell us everything you were doing that night at the Gateway."

"I told you. I was trying to break in. I didn't see a soul. There was only me there."

"Where exactly were you trying to break in?" "Round the back. I thought I might get in through a window. They had them locked up tight."

"Yeah right. Take him back to his cell."

He is hauled off hollering obscenities, proclaiming his innocence, every step of the way. Angus Runcie has pulled himself and his dignity together enough to say, "You are a menace to society. I will be issuing a complaint when I return to my office."

"Please do. I can't wait until I read it. Another critically acclaimed work of fiction from the pen of Angus Runcie, Lawyer to the underworld."

"Iain, when you were at the Gateway did you check for fingerprints round the back."

"No, Ma'am. Have you seen the size of the Gateway? I'd still be at it yet."

"Go and do it now. Take Roy, Jason and Abigail with you. See if Brian Gevers is free to help. That should speed things up. Pay particular attention to doors and windows."

On his return to the station Iain says, "As you can imagine there were a lot, but not as many as I thought. The windows are pretty high up so not many people would be able to reach them."

"Do any of them match Shawn Ratray's?"

"They do, Ma'am."

"Looks like he was telling the truth about what he was up to."

"It would be the first time ever that he has," says Jason. "I came across him a lot in uniform and if lying was an Olympic sport he'd win Gold."

"To be honest I don't think he's our killer anyway. Despite the family connection to the undertakers, he hasn't got the finesse required of our killer."

"twenty quid says you're right," says Nina.

"What a day. Who's coming to the pub?"

A fire wouldn't have got them out of the building any quicker.

13

The worker methodically gathers together the tools of his trade. First a pristine metal trolley, polished and gleaming, reflecting the brilliance of the sunbeams dancing through the window. Next, a white linen cloth is draped over the trolley and smoothed. Not a crease to be seen. A scalpel is tenderly freed from its covering and placed on the cloth, and is joined by surgical ligatures. A bottle of strong disinfectant and six swabs are next in line. A scrupulously clean machine and some tubing are lined up on the lower shelf of the trolley. A cannula and a pair of cannula forceps, trocar and cotton wool completes the line up.

The worker surveys the equipment. One large hand reaches out and moves the trocar a few millimetres to the right. He looks again. Nods. Now all is ready.

14

Shona is dreaming of being eaten alive by giant leaches. For once the ringing phone is a welcome interruption. Shakespeare is stretched out lying so close to her that the leaches make perfect sense. She is annoyed at Shona's movement and bats her with a paw.

"Sorry kitty cat."

Shakespeare opens one eye. Her look says, call me that again and you'll be missing your larynx. Shona fumbles for the phone.

"McKenzie."

"Ma'am. I'm sorry to be the bearer of bad news…"

"Where's the body this time?"

"The ruins of St. Andrews cathedral in St Andrews."

"St Andrews isn't mine. Tell Fife to deal with their own dead bodies." She pauses in the act of putting the phone down. The Duty Sergeant is saying, "Ma'am, Ma'am, don't hang up."

"What?"

"They said to tell you the body is definitely yours."

"Why is every body in Scotland automatically thrown in my direction?"

"No clue Ma'am. Perhaps because they usually have something to do with you."

"Thank you for the cheery words. Tell them I'm on my way."

Forty minutes, and a grande double skinny latte later, Shona is standing at the crime scene. She is peering down at a monk artfully displayed in an ancient stone casket. A beautifully executed cross is carved on his chest. The casket, in turn, is inside a burial pit. Peter, sporting six stitches and a large lump on his head is beside her.

"We've moved from vicars to monks. It'll be a long time since this contained a dead body."

"I'm sure you're right. How on earth did they manage this little feat? Doesn't this place have security alarms up the ying yang?"

"I'm no' sure but we can ask the caretaker. He's standing over there. He came in early to set up for a film crew that are coming in."

"They'll probably want us out and the original occupant back in. I think the skeleton's part of the National Museums of Scotland's inventory."

"How on earth did you know that. Never mind, you seem to know everything about Scotland, never mind Dundee. I'm off to speak to the caretaker."

The caretaker, a man in his mid twenties, is leaning up against a nine hundred year old wall, smoking a cigarette. Shona is sure that's against the terms and conditions of his contract. However, she is more worried about her crime scene. She flashes her badge. "Detective Inspector McKenzie. Put that out. You could be destroying evidence."

The man looks sulky but goes to stub the cigarette out on the wall.

"You've got to be kidding me. Use something more suitable."

Once the cigarette is out and stowed in the pocket of his strategically ripped jeans, Shona asks his name.

"Paul Peterson."

"Could you tell me how you found the body, Mr Peterson?"

"I came in early to set up for a film crew. They're shooting some telly series about a couple of ancient monks who investigate crimes." He stops talking.

"And?"

"They wanted to shoot this area in particular. I was asked to run electricity cables across to here. When I got the first cable here I found this." His lower lip trembles. Not as brave as he seems thinks Shona.

"Did you see anything, or touch anything Mr Peterson?"

"Not on your life. I just pulled out my mobile and rang you lot."

"Do you have the name of the film company?"

"No, but you can ask them yourself. They'll be here soon."

Shona wipes away the sweat trickling down her neck. There's not an inch of shade to be found in the cathedral and the day is already doing a good impression of the Sahara desert.

"Do you have a key to the visitors centre?"

"Yes."

"Go with my Sergeant and open it up. He'll interview you in there. We'll need to use it as a base of operations for the day."

By the time she returns, Sergeant Muir, the POLSA has a large tent up over the burial pit. A good job thinks Shona. In this heat their victim will either be burnt to a crisp or mummified. The remainder of the team are standing just outside the tent looking like they had nothing to do.

"Good of you to join us. I suppose you two were too busy choosing your designer wardrobe to tip up any earlier." She waves a hand at Nina and Roy.

"We wouldn't like to let the team down by coming half dressed."

"If the team was about sartorial elegance then you pair would be heading it up. However, you may have forgotten it's about solving grizzly murders. Get in the tent."

They all gaze at the coffin then each other.

"At least this one seems a bit cleaner," says Abigail.

Iain, who is wielding his Canon and a lens the size of Scotland, adds, "and a lot less smelly."

"I wonder about you lot sometimes. I'm sure the poor sods who have been murdered didn't have time to shower and put on the latest Hugo Boss fragrance."

"That's more than can be said about Roy," says Jason. "He smells like a girl."

"You could do with looking after your appearance a bit more. You're not on patrol in Afghanistan now."

"Boys, stop the squabbling. It's wearing thin. Abigail, take Roy and do a search of the north side of the Cathedral. Nina and I will do the south side. See if there's anywhere someone could have got in."

"What about me?" asks Jason.

"Go and help Peter. Don't let him do too much. He shouldn't be back at work yet."

"Trust you to get the easy job Soldier Boy."

"Roy, I'm warning you. Move now before I arrest you."

"What for?"

"I'll think of something."

Shona and Nina wait until Larry Briar, the police surgeon arrives. They get a surprise when Whitney Williams flies in amongst a waft of Gucci Guilty. Whitney is the Police Surgeon from Perthshire and she looks like a waif. She is as small as Larry is large, and is much more effervescent than the taciturn Larry. She is an unexpected breath of fresh air.

"Whitney. What brings you to St Andrews? You're usually plying your wares in the country."

"Larry's on holiday for a month so I'm covering. I expect I'll be seeing a lot of you the way you collect murders."

Even Whitney, whom she's barely met, thinks Shona is Genghis Khan. Shona takes it in her stride.

"Hopefully not, Whitney, but I can't promise anything."

Whitney's tinkling laugh rings out over the Cathedral. It is infectious.

"Show me to the body Shona and I'll give you my considered opinion."

"Trust me, you won't need to consider it much."

"Why would anyone carve a cross on a monk's chest?" asks Whitney when she sees the deceased.

"Haven't a clue. I was hoping you might have an inkling."

"I don't think I've ever seen a dead vicar, never mind one with a carving. I can certify this one is dead without a shadow of a doubt. There's not much blood though."

"That might be because he's been drained of blood. According to Mary that's what happened to the last one."

"You mean there are others?"

"Only two others. Things aren't that bad - yet."

"Shona, you're a positive wonder. I'm looking forward to working with you. I'll never know what's coming along next."

"Nothing I hope," but the perfumed dervish has disappeared leaving Shona speaking to the still morning air.

It is almost soporific walking around the walls of the

ancient Cathedral. Wild flowers cling to the stones and bees buzz around their heads. The sea sparkles at the bottom of rugged cliffs.

"I bet you're glad you came back to Scotland. You wouldn't get a view like this in Oxford."

"There are a fair few old buildings there you know. They're just a little more habitable."

Nina's laugh is carried out, on a ripple of a breeze, towards the sea.

"If anyone on a ship hears you they'll think you're a siren luring them to their death on the rocks."

"You've got an overactive imagination, Ma'am."

Shona stops. "They could have got in here. There's a gap where a small portion of wall has broken down".

"Those stones look like they've been placed there." Nina points to a small mound. "It's a dry stane dyke so it would be easy to take it down.'

"A what?"

"A dry stone wall. There's no cement, just stones laid one on top of the other."

Shona steps through the wall to an area of grass which looks flatter than the rest. "The body could have been laid here whilst our dumpee did their impression of a brickie. Go and get Iain and his camera."

Shona is looking critically around the area when she spots something. She bends down to look closely at the gap in the wall. There is a small patch of what looks like blood on a jagged stone. Then she hears the voice which makes her brain melt.

"Shona does it again."

"Douglas." She takes the opportunity to kiss him given there are no witnesses and she is some distance from the body.

"Don't mind us. You pair just recreate the love scene from Romeo and Juliet."

They break apart, Shona's face red. "Everyone's a comic. Haven't you something better to do than ogle Douglas and me?"

"I was escorting Iain over here. Good job too. The poor lad wouldn't know what had hit him."

"Don't drag me into this. I'll get started with the photos."

"I think there's blood on the stone. Have you got a swab with you?"

"Yep. I'll photograph and scrape some of it off."

"You could start with a photo of the Inspector and the Procurator Fiscal. I'm sure *The Courier* would pay good money for that. Canoodling over a dead body."

"Sergeant Chakrabarti I'm putting you in for a transfer. I hear Benbecula are looking for a volunteer."

"Benbecula couldn't cope with me, Ma'am."

"Much as I'd like to listen to this witty repartee all day, could someone brief me on what's happening?" Douglas interrupts.

"Sorry Douglas. Have you seen our latest victim?"

"No, your guys herded me in your direction."

"Follow me. Nina, carry on with the patrol."

Douglas gazes down at the monk, looking pensive. "Embalmed monks don't come along very often. Not in this day and age anyway."

"I suppose he goes well with the dead vicars."

"Why would anyone want to kill a vicar?"

"I'm not sure. I think it could be some sort of satanic ritual. It could also be someone getting their own back for childhood sexual abuse."

"It's a bit extreme."

"I'm ready to clutch at anything never mind the wind. It's as good a theory as any of the others we've come up with."

"What denomination is the costume."

"Not a clue. I'm determined to find out though."

"I'll leave you to your ferreting. See you soon no doubt." Douglas, his dreamy voice and smiling eyes walk off. Shona felt a little less jolly than she had a few minutes ago. She doesn't have time to feel blue for very long.

"Ma'am, the film crew are here and they're not happy," says Roy.

"What are you doing here? You're meant to be inspecting the perimeter."

"We're finished."

"Already. It was meant to be a search not a route march."

"Ask Abigail. We did it properly."

"I would if she was anywhere to be seen."

"She's gone to the shop to get bottles of water. We're dying of heat exhaustion, Ma'am."

"Fair enough. Come with me and we'll sort the film crew out."

"We've paid thousands of pounds to film here today. Be a sweetheart and let us in."

"No. The blue tape should tell you quite clearly that it's a crime scene."

"Sweetie, we need the early morning light. The main characters are praying outside."

"Call me sweetie once more and you won't need to hire an actor to play the next dead body in your movie."

"Do you know who I am?"

"I haven't a clue, but if you continue to annoy me I will be finding out when the pair of us are in an interview room. Now, I will need to interview everyone here. My Constable will take you all to the visitors centre."

"What about our filming?"

"Do I look like I'm worried about your film schedule? The quicker we all get on the quicker we'll be able to release the area back to you. Now move."

Four hours and twenty dead ends later the team are back at Bell Street. They are hot, frazzled, hungry and no further forward.

"I need a bacon roll."

"What you need and what you're going to get are two different things."

"I'm a grown man. You cannae tell me what I can have to eat."

"No, but your wife can. Come on. Let's see if Annie or Doreen is on. I'm sure one of them will grill you some bacon and do you a couple of poached eggs."

"Aye. That would be just the ticket."

"The rest of you are having the healthy version as well."

"What?"

"Stop moaning. It'll do you good. Like the three musketeers we stick together."

"That wasn't half bad, Ma'am. Without all that grease you can really taste the bacon," says Nina.

"Enough talk of dead pigs. What about our dead bodies?"

"I think we can rule out the luvvies. They were all getting down with the groove at the student union," says Roy.

"How did they get in there?" asks Shona. "Most of them would need a telescope to see forty again."

"It's the only nightclub in town. Plus film crew can weasel their way in anywhere."

"You're right. I still want them looked at. They could be doing this for publicity."

"Do you no' think that's taking publicity a bit too far."

"This is the glitterati we're talking about. They'd do

anything to get themselves noticed. Roy, I want you to dig deep, especially into the Director, Randy Sutcliffe. He's a sycophantic misogynist, and with a name like Sutcliffe he's right at the top of my suspect list."

"Just because Peter Sutcliffe caused havoc, it doesn't mean everyone with that name is dodgy."

"The Yorkshire Ripper? Do you think it might be a copycat, or a relative of his who is taking hero worship too far?" asks Abigail.

"Nothing would surprise me. Get on to it Roy. If there's any chance they're related then arrest him."

"You can't arrest someone because he has the name of a serial killer," says Peter.

"Don't you think I know that? We can keep him safely ensconced in a cell for a couple of days whilst we check it all out."

When Shona returns to her desk the Chief calls her in.

"DI McKenzie. Why is it that you can't get through a case without a complaint coming in?"

"What's it about this time, Sir?"

"Angus Runcie says that you were threatening his client."

"I did no such thing, Sir. I feel I behaved myself with great restraint and decorum."

"I don't believe a word of it. Did you stay this side of the law?"

"Of course I did."

"Stop annoying every person you come into contact with. Do your job without threats, veiled or otherwise. You seem to have missed the part in your training which says we are here to uphold the law, not break it."

"Sir," but she is talking to a bald head.

"Sir."

"What? I have better things to do than talk to you."

"We have had another murder." His stare does not bode well for her future. She outlines the developments in the case.

"St Andrews? It would seem every force in Scotland thinks we are at their beck and call. Can't they do their own work?"

"In all fairness, Sir, we are Police Scotland now. Also, this body did suggest it might be part of my case."

"Why do you always have to argue with me Inspector? Get this case solved and do it quickly."

Shona is left thinking that the Chief's dead body would look nice in the stone coffin next to their victim.

Shona interrupts Peter in the act of reading that morning's *Courier*.

"You're coming with me. It's time to pay a visit to Dodgy, Dishonest and Dubious, funeral directors to the scum."

"What? Do you mean Claypotts, Ratray and Elgin?"

"Of course that's what I mean. Surely Dundee can't have more than one dodgy undertaker."

"I think your version's better, Ma'am. Sums them up well."

"We'll take Jason as well. The way our investigations go, he might come in useful as a bodyguard."

Shona has no clue whether she is speaking to Ratray or Elgin. Slick Andra is nowhere to be seen. Whichever partner it is, they are refusing to play ball.

"Peter, Jason, don't let anyone move a muscle until I get back here with a warrant."

"Right you are, Ma'am." One of the staff starts to rise. "You heard the DI, sit down and look busy."

Three quarters of an hour later she is back with a warrant. The Sherriff was smiling when he handed it over. "We've been trying to get that lot for years. They're slippery as Satan and twice as wily."

"You're interfering with the running of our business. We have work to do."

Shona has worked out this particular pile of slime is Elgin.

"Mr Elgin, most of your clients are dead. They're not exactly going anywhere. Unless of course you're expecting a re-creation of the resurrection?"

"This is a serious business. We need to attend to the dead."

"I appreciate the sanctity of what you do in here Mr Elgin. We will conduct our search with due gravitas and decorum. We don't want to dishonour the dead or add to the grief of their loved ones. Now please can we do our search?"

Mr Elgin stands back and waves them through. Shona, true to her word, reigns her natural instincts in and conducts the search quietly. Every nook and cranny is explored and they find nothing. Mr Elgin who keeps his evil eye on them the whole way escorts them.

"Can we please see your records?"

"No. They are confidential."

"Once they're dead there's no longer a confidentiality issue. Plus if you look at our warrant in detail, it says we can search your records."

"I hadn't expected such actions from an officer of the law. I imagined you were above reproach. It would seem that is not so."

"Save us the false platitudes and toddle off and fetch the records. DC Roberts will escort you."

The records indicate every body is accounted for. Shona whispers to Peter, "They all seem above board. Might be worth doing a raid later just to make sure they don't sneak an extra one in."

"Knowing this lot like I do I'd have tae agree."

15

For once the Chief is lost for words. There is silence for a good two minutes and then, "You want to do what? I know you bring a new level of madness to my job, but you have surpassed yourself."

"I appreciate it might seem somewhat flaky, Sir, but I think it's important. If we do a raid we can see if they are keeping any extra bodies in there."

Shaking his head the Chief says, "I can't believe I'm agreeing to this. We had none of these shenanigans before you returned to Dundee. Are you sure Oxford wouldn't like you back?"

"I don't think so, Sir. They seemed quite happy at the thought of my moving to Scotland." Shona grins and the Chief can't help but respond.

"I'm sure they were ecstatic. Do your raid, but for Pete's sake, Shona, do it as respectfully as you can."

"Of course, Sir. I wouldn't have it any other way."

"Why don't I believe you?"

The team are equally as surprised.

"A raid? On a funeral parlour?" Are you sure that's a good idea?" asks Nina.

"There's no way I'm going into a funeral parlour at night," says Roy. "It's way too creepy."

"I'm with Roy," adds Jason. "Nobody goes into a funeral parlour at night."

"I'm Chinese. We are taught to honour the dead," says Abigail. "We shouldn't be disturbing them."

"Oh for heavens sake. Abigail you're excused for

cultural reasons. Peter, your head injury excuses you. Everyone else is coming on the raid. I'll see if Brian Gevers would like to join us. I'm sure a strong lad like him won't be frightened of a few dead bodies."

"I'm not frightened. Count me in"

"Me, scared. Never. I'll be leading the charge."

Roy and Jason speak together.

"I'll come as well Ma'am," says Abigail. "It doesn't seem quite fair to the rest of them."

"It's up to you. Go home and grab something to eat. We'll meet back here at 2000 hours to plan and get kitted out."

"Will we be carrying guns?" asks Roy."

"Yes."

Roy and Jason high five. "I love my job," says Roy.

"Oi, Jesse James. Cool it. You're not to go waving guns about indiscriminately. I can just see the headlines in *The Courier* if you shoot a corpse."

"Are you taking a battering ram, ma'am?" asks Iain.

"What on earth for? It's an undertakers, not a drug den," says Shona.

"We'll need to break the door down."

"I'm going to pick the lock? I've already arranged with the alarm company to shut down the alarm."

"Were you a criminal in a previous life? Where on earth did you learn all that?" asks Nina.

"You don't get to the rank of Inspector without picking up a few tricks along the way."

"Remind me never to do anything wrong. I'd hate to be on the wrong side of you," says Jason.

"When you're all quite finished discussing my criminal sideline maybe you could get ready to raid, Dingy, Dodgy and Dreary Esquire. We'll get there at 2230. It should be dark enough for them to be dealing in 'off the book' bodies."

"You have an original turn of phrase, if you don't mind me saying so, Ma'am." says Abigail."

"You might want to be careful about what you say in Dundee. Everybody knows everyone around here," says Iain.

"Don't tell me any of you lot are related to Pa Broon, Russian thugs or any undertaker within a fifty mile radius of here?" says Shona.

"My uncle and cousin are undertakers. Long established family business," says Jason.

"And you didn't think to mention this?"

"Never thought of it. They're fine upstanding citizens. Never broke the law in their lives."

Shona just shakes her head.

The lock is picked and they spread out around the dark rooms. Nothing seems to be out of place. All is as they left it that morning. Then, Roy turns his torch towards a cluttered corner, and screams. Clearly displayed is a partially dressed young woman and slick Andra. The woman takes one look and adds her screams to those of Roy.

"Are they coffins? Where've you brought me? Who are you lot?"

"Why are you in my funeral parlour at this time of night? This is an abuse of police power."

"A funeral parlour! OMG I've gotta get out of here.."

"Shut up Roy." Shona turns to the woman. "We're the police." She shines the torch on her badge.

Bursting into tears she gathers her clothes and heads towards the door.

"Not so fast miss. We need to talk to you. What's your name?"

"Kylie Brown."

"You're not related to George Brown are you?"

"He's my Granddad. Why?"

You have got to be kidding me thinks Shona. Of all the kids in Dundee slick Andra could have taken up with, she had to be a part of the Brown Family.

"How old are you Kylie?"

"Sixteen."

Shona waves Nina forward. "My Sergeant will take you to the station and your Granddad can pick you up there."

"Am I being arrested? I haven't done anything. My Dad'll kill me." Sobs shake her slight body.

Shona is gentle. "You're not in trouble. We just want to keep you safe."

Nina leads her away. "You can call me Nina. What school do you go to?" Nina's voice fades as they leave.

"Right sonny Jim, you're coming with us," says Shona.

"You can't arrest me. I haven't done anything."

"We'll discuss that down at the station. We'll also discuss what your husband and kid are going to think of you sleeping with girls."

"Don't tell Francois. He'll kill me."

"If you swing both ways then you might find you need to let your nearest and dearest know about it. I'm sure they'll find out soon enough."

"I dinnae think your boyfriend's called Francoise. More likely tae be Francis. We'll need his real name so we can contact him."

"Peter, don't torment the prisoner."

Peter grins.

"If the girl's sixteen then under Scottish Law it isn't an offence for him to have sex with her," says Nina when they are back in the office.

"You're right, but he is a lot older than her. I want

to find out if he was in a position of trust. If that's so, then it is an offence."

"How are we going to do that?"

"Ask her, and if necessary ask Pa Broon."

"George Brown will kill Andra," says Abigail.

"I'm well aware of that. Hence the reason Andra's cooling his jets in a cell instead of roaming the streets of Dundee."

Kylie breaks the news that slick Andra is a friend of her father. They got to know each other and fell in love. Shona has grounds for arrest.

"Maybe Andra should have thought about the consequences before suddenly falling in love with a wee girl instead of a man," says Shona. Kylie has been taken off for a drink and a cake or two. The rest of the station is still awash in calories despite the ban in CID.

Arrest is the least of Andra's worries when George Brown and Kylie's Dad turn up.

"Why have you arrested my Granddaughter?"

"We haven't arrested her Mr Brown. We are merely keeping her safe." Shona explains the situation without mentioning Andra's name.

"Whoever did this is dead. When I get my hands on him he will be begging for mercy."

"Mr Brown, I appreciate that you are upset but issuing threats in a police station is not one of your better moves. I will turn a blind eye this once. Now take your granddaughter home."

After telling Andra that he is in for the night while they investigate, Shona wends her weary way home. She's had a bellyful of undertakers one way or another.

"Shakespeare, if you ever leave me, don't move in with an undertaker."

The cat purrs and rubs up against Shona's arm. She

seems to be saying I could never leave you. Shona thinks she is probably saying where's my food. The food dispensed, Shona falls asleep on the couch. She doesn't even feed herself.

16

The room is ready. The caretaker wheels in the body. It is moved onto the stone table and the limbs carefully arranged. One step back and he gazes critically at the figure before him. It is filthy and unkempt. Matted hair, broken, dirt filled nails and a foul smell which emanates from the mouth.

Several urns containing boiling water stand by. Alongside them is a large bottle of Swarfega - a liquid soap - and a large quantity of cloths. A sizeable china basin is filled with the boiling water. The caretaker pulls on surgical gloves, two pairs, which fit his hands like another layer of skin. He smooths the left one to eradicate an errant crease. Satisfied he twists the lid from a fresh bottle of cold water and adds it to the bowl. He tests it to make sure it is just the right temperature.

Swarfega is poured slowly onto the man's body. Not a drop more than is needed. The body is vigorously washed with a cloth. Every single millimetre is covered, not a hair left untouched. The caretaker rinses and repeats. Rinses and repeats. The filthy water is poured down the drain. The bowl is cleaned thoroughly and polished dry. Then the routine starts again. In the end every inch of the body is clean. The hair is washed and brushed. Fingernails are cut and cleaned. The caretaker steps back and surveys his handiwork. He moves a few errant hairs. Makes sure they are in place. He looks again and nods just once. He is happy with his handiwork. The body is immaculate and ready for the next stage. It is covered with a sheet and left for the next player to attend to his task. In this heat it will not be long.

Before he leaves the caretaker cleans the room. Every surface is cleaned and lovingly polished. The trolley is buffed to a high shine. Another pristine trolley is brought forward. The room is ready. The caretaker's eyes sweep the room. He nods again and walks out of the door.

17

Having spent the night on the sofa, Shona is tired and cranky in the morning. She is not in the mood to deal with Andra and his obnoxious lawyer.

"You seem a wee bit out of sorts, Ma'am, if you don't mind me saying," says Peter

"I do mind you saying. We need to get going on this. Has Andra asked for a lawyer?"

"He has and your no' going to like it."

Don't tell me it's Angus Runcie."

"Worse. It's Margaret McCluskey."

"I need a couple of large coffees and sustenance before I face Margaret McCluskey. You and I are off to the canteen." She hurries off with Peter happily ambling behind.

A now rejuvenated Shona strides into the interview room, and slams down a file on the desk. Slick Andra jumps and even the tank McCluskey looks more than a little startled.

"Interview with Andrew Claypotts, DI Shona McKenzie, DS Peter Johnston and Margaret McCluskey in attendance."

"Why was I not informed of my client's arrest last night?"

"Because it was one o'clock in the morning. Are you like a taxi driver and get extra money after midnight or something?" says Shona.

"How dare you talk to me like that?"

"Grief. I haven't got going yet. Can I ask your client some questions? We might all get out of here before knocking off time. We're not all being paid by the hour."

"That is…"

"Mr Claypotts do you know why you were arrested?"

"No."

"That's funny because we clearly told you last night. You were arrested for having sex with an underage girl."

"Underage? She's sixteen."

"My client is right. The age for consensual sex is sixteen in Scotland."

"If you're as good a lawyer as you say you are, then you must know about position of trust."

"That doesn't affect my client."

"He's Kylie's father's best friend." Shona stops to gain her composure. "Apart from that he's thirty years older than the girl. It's obscene. It's bordering on paedophilia if you ask me."

"Are you saying my client is a paedophile?" McLuskey is busy taking notes.

"I'm not going to spend the morning arguing with you pair about the finer points of the law. Let's see what the courts think. Now just so we've got things clear - Andrew Claypotts I am arresting you under Section 6 (Indecent Behaviour Towards a Girl between 12 and 16) of the Criminal Law (Consolidation) (Scotland) Act 1995, for procuring sex with a girl under the age of eighteen with whom you are in a position of trust."

For once Shona manages to complete the interview with no chaos or disruption. Unless you count an aggrieved, "Humph," from Margaret McLuskey, as a disruption. Shona is happy to discount that one. The Chief will be pleased.

Roy is hard at it. There is almost an inferno coming from his computer.

"What's got you so excited about your work?" asks Shona.

"I'm looking to see if there is any connection between the dead men, apart from the fact that they're all vicars. I'm using the photos and cross referencing them."

"Well not quite all vicars as one of them is Catholic, but we won't argue. Any joy?"

"Not so far, but I'm sure I'll come up with something." He turns back to the keyboard and peers intently at his 27 inch iMac screen. When it comes to computers Roy is a station legend. Not even the Chief quibbled about the cost of his computer.

Shona grabs the remainder of the team, who gather around Peter's desk.

"I'm beginning to think the undertaker angle isn't getting us anywhere."

"I think you're right Ma'am. But who else would know about embalming?" asks Abigail.

"You're guess is as good as mine. What about taxidermists? Do they use embalming techniques?"

Blank stares provide her answer. "Okay. Abigail find out what a taxidermist does. Go and visit one if necessary."

"What about doctors? Do they do anything about embalming during their training?" says Jason.

"Good point. Go find out."

"Nina, do a search on trades which would use embalming, or at least have a good working knowledge of the process."

"Consider it done." Nina and her contagious smile disappear.

"Iain, use your contacts to find out if they know of any similar cases. Peter, you and I are going to search

HOLMES for embalmed corpses."

Peace descends and Shona returns to her office with a fortifying, freshly brewed Cuban coffee. Her Grandmother had brought her several bags back from a trip to the country. Shona often wonders why her Grandmother has a better time than she does. She inhales the aromatic blend and sighs. Five minutes peace. Bliss. Then with one click of the mouse she is off on a wild ride through HOLMES.

An hour and twenty minutes later she has drunk three cups of coffee and her friend HOLMES has come up blank.

"Three million quid on a computer programme and not one hit in the whole of the UK."

"Talking to yourself are you, Ma'am. I'm no' surprised there's nothing on HOLMES. There's only you manages to collect all these daft murders." Peter is standing at the door.

"Thanks for the vote of confidence."

"You're blazing a trail, Ma'am. In years to come when they're looking for wacky murders, your name will be right at the top, dancing in neon lights."

"I don't know whether that's a good thing or a bad. If we don't solve these murders then it will be worse than bad. Did you come up with anything?"

"Not a dicky bird."

"I can't believe no one has come forward to identify our dead vicars either. Surely, a church would notice they were missing their spiritual leader?"

"Aye you'd think so. Unless they were up to high jinks. The congregation might have murdered them to get rid of them."

"I could stretch my imagination to that being true for one case. But three? A bit more than a coincidence don't you think?"

"Aye." Peter's shoulders droop.

"How's the head Peter. Not giving you too much gyp I hope? You can go home if you would like a rest."

"I'm fine here. At least the wife cannae go on at me about healthy eating when I'm at work."

"Let me know if you need some time to yourself. In the meantime, grab the others and we'll meet in the briefing room."

"Have any of the searches thrown anything up?"

"Not a thing in my case," says Roy. "There's not a photo of our men anywhere to be found."

"Have you tried the deepest, darkest reaches," asks Shona.

"They're vicars, Ma'am. I don't think they're likely to be down there with the bottom feeders."

"Assume nothing, Roy. Treat them the same as any other victim. Remember our last case."

"Fair enough. I wouldn't have imagined any shenanigans then either."

"You've obviously led a sheltered life."

"Not a bit of it. I could tell you some tales."

"Spare me the details. Get those fingers working like a typist on speed."

"Can I go anywhere?"

"Absolutely. As long as it doesn't involve a first class ticket to Australia. Abigail, what have you got?"

"I phoned a taxidermist. The nearest one is Edinburgh. We don't appear to be big on stuffing dead animals in Dundee."

"Surely that's a good thing," says Roy. "Stuffing Fido when he dies is a bit weird."

"Each to their own, Roy. Let Abigail speak."

"They do use embalming but only to a certain extent. They use formaldehyde in the feet of dogs and in the carpal joint of a wing."

"Not quite body filling levels then. I'm not sure they'd have the equipment needed for a whole body," says Shona.

"I'm no' sure they'd be coming all the way from Edinburgh to dump the body either. They've enough churches in their own City to be using as a final resting place."

"Good point, Peter. Well made. I'm sure you're right."

"Jason, do Doctors learn embalming?"

"They do, Ma'am. Well, they sort of do."

"They either do or they don't Jason. For goodness sake get on with it. The whole ecclesiastical community of Dundee could be dead before you make up your mind."

"They use soft fix embalming to prepare cadavers. Doctors can then practice surgery on them. They use a solution of salts, antiseptic boric acid, ethylene glycol, antifreeze, and a very low level of formaldehyde. They use red dye though to make the blood look real. Our guys are definitely colourless so I don't think that was used."

"I would agree, so we are back to the undertakers. The cross makes me think it might be some sort of satanic sacrifice. Anyone here got any experience with that?"

"Ma'am, I know we're all a bit weird but even we draw the line at sacrificing humans to the temple of the occult," says Nina.

Through gales of laughter a red faced Shona says, "You know that's not what I mean. Go and research it. Anyone not working hard within three minutes is being seconded to traffic."

This galvanizes the troops and most dash towards computers. Abigail stays put.

"Something on your mind Sergeant?"

"I thought maybe the University Library may have books in their collection which would throw some light on the matter. I know the Internet's the cat's meow, but it doesn't contain every bit of information in the world."

"I like the colour of your thinking. Would you like to take anyone with you?"

"Peter might want to break out of the shackles. The library might be a bit cooler. They've probably got air conditioners."

"Off the pair of you go then. The rest of us can just cook slowly on a medium gas."

Shona is sitting in a puddle of sweat and losing the will to live. She is also fast reevaluating her choice of a leather chair. When she chose it, in the middle of a Dundee blizzard, she'd never imagined a heat wave. Standing, she heads towards the kitchen. She'd let a jug of coffee go cold and decides to add some ice. Caffeine and coolness at once seemed to be a winner. Until she takes the first mouthful then promptly spits it into the sink.

"Is that a new mouthwash, Ma'am?" says Roy behind her.

"Do you know how to make iced coffee, Roy?"

"Do I look like an iced coffee kind of guy? I drink double shot espresso. Look online. There'll be millions of recipes on there."

"No wonder you're wired."

After discovering that she neither has the time, nor the equipment to make proper iced coffee, Shona falls back on the hot version. She takes it in to the main office where everyone seems to be occupied.

"Are you lot on Facebook, or are you doing research?"

"I never want to look at another site on satanic

worship as long as I live. How can there be so much info out there about the occult? The web's almost exploding with it." says Nina.

"Anything about carving crosses on victims?"

"Apart from some weirdos who brand themselves, or carve themselves for body art, then no. Nothing seems to be linked to the occult. In fact most experts say that Ritual Satanic Abuse was a myth widely believed in the 80's and 90's. Nothing more recent."

"I'll do a search on it on HOLMES. You guys keep rifling through the Interweb. Let me know when my disappearing Sergeants return. I swear they could have read every book in the uni library by now."

"They're probably sitting in an air conditioned café somewhere."

"They're going to need air conditioning in their graves when I get hold of them."

"Sergeant Johnston and Sergeant Lau, nice of you to grace us with your presence. Had a pleasant day out have you?"

"There was hardly anything in the University library, so we went to the Central library. The public library's better than the uni one," says Abigail.

"That's somewhat comforting. I'd hate to think we were running degrees in occult practice. So did your little jaunt come up with anything."

"M Hai as they say in Cantonese. In English it's no."

"I've enough problems translating Scottish without you adding Cantonese into the mix."

"Sorry, Ma'am."

"You're not sorry at all. I take it you pair spent some time being fed and watered? Peter, if you went anywhere near a cream cake I'm telling your wife."

"I didnae. I swear. It's no' worth it. The missus

would skin me alive."

"At least you'd lose weight then, " says Jason.

"Ha, flaming, ha. Remember I'm your senior and can make you do all the scut work."

"You do that whether I make jokes or not, so I might as well have some fun."

"Gentlemen. If you please. I've come up with a couple of leads from HOLMES. One is in Liverpool and the other in Dublin. I'm going to give them a ring. The rest of you can go home. Back here nice and sharp in the morning."

Shona is soon through to her counterpart, Terry Derrick, in Liverpool.

"Go'ed Lass. What can I do for you?"

"A couple of years back you had three murders that looked like they were linked to the occult. Did anything come of the investigation?"

"It all went quiet. We thought our lad might have moved. What have you got?"

"Did your victims have a cross carved on their chest?"

"Did you say a cross? On their chest?"

"I certainly did."

After about a minutes silence Terry says, "No. No crosses. Multiple burns with what could have been a hot poker. Never caught him. He was wrecking our heads."

"He was obviously wrecking his victims' as well. I'm wondering if it's the same killer and they've escalated?"

"Could be. Would you like me to send you the notes?"

"That would be great. Thanks."

"Ta'ra now. Hope you catch your killer."

The conversation with Dublin goes much the same, but with an Irish accent instead of Liverpudlian. This time the victims were women and suffered genital mutilation. Shona puts the phone down wondering if they are all linked.

She grabs her handbag ready to leave for the night. The lights are still on in the main office. Thinking it is Mo, the cleaner, she goes in to thank her for the plant. Mo is nowhere to be seen but Roy is at his computer.

"Why are you still here?"

"I might have something on one of our vicars. I want to check out every single parameter before I give a definitive yes. I'll carry on and you'll have the details first thing."

"I'm impressed. Thanks, Roy," but he had turned back to his screen.

18

As the saying goes, the best laid plans of mice and men often go wrong, thinks Shona. Well Robert Burns didn't quite say that but she never could get her tongue around the Scottish version. Instead of discussing Roy's miraculous discovery, she's standing at the door of St Boniface Church in Dundee at 4.45 a.m. At her feet is the body of a dead nun with a cross tattooed on her chest. Peter arrived before her and is gazing at the nun.

"That's no way for a nun to finish up, Ma'am. Her chest is open for all to see."

"I know, Peter, but we can't disturb evidence. The POLSA will have a tent up soon enough. I've never seen a nun with a tattoo of a spider on her breast before."

"Seen many nun's breasts have you, Ma'am?"

"Funnily enough, none."

"If this lassie is a nun then she must have been imported. I don't recognise her and we met all the nuns in the convent in our last case." He pauses, then, "Yon young lassie over there found her." He points to a girl who looks to be about fifteen years old. She's holding herself and shivering despite the heat.

"What's she doing out at this time of the morning?"

"She's a cleaner in the Overgate. She was taking a shortcut to get there." He interprets her puzzled look. "She says she's twenty."

"I'll go and speak to her. Move all these waifs and strays out of the way. They're mucking up my crime scene."

"They're not waifs and strays, they're beat bobbies."

"They're still cluttering up my crime scene." She pauses, then raises her voice. "Oi, you lot. Move back. Any evidence is going to be stuck to your size twelves."

"We do know what we're doing Ma'am." One young PC is obviously feeling brave.

Peter steps in before Shona launches an attack. "Okay boys. You heard the DI. Move back a bit."

There's a lot of muttering but they all hurry back out to the road. Most of them know Shona well enough that they don't want to get on the wrong side of her. She heard one of them say to the previously brave copper. "She's a legend around here. Don't argue with her. She might put you in a hole with one of the bodies she collects."

She smiles and says, "Very well put."

The young witness is Jessica Hamley. "I…I… I can't believe what I saw. Wh…why would anyone do that?" She starts to cry.

"We don't know yet Jessica. But I can assure you we intend to find out. It will help us if you will answer a few questions."

"Will I have to be a witness? Will the person who did this come after me," she says, eyes wide and darting everywhere.

"No one is going to come after you Jessica. We'll see to that."

"Jess. Everyone calls me Jess."

"What time did you see the body?"

"About 4 o'clock. I phoned straight away."

"I'm sure you did. How did you happen to notice it?"

"My phone rang, and when I turned to answer it I saw something. I thought it was someone who had fallen over and might need help. I'm doing my medical training so went over to see if I could help."

What is it about all these medics, thinks Shona. They all seem to fall apart the minute they see a dead body. You'd think they'd be able to cope a bit better.

"Did you touch anything?"

"The nun's neck. I wanted to see if she was still alive."

What! A blind man could see at a hundred yards the nun was a goner. What do they teach medical students these days, Shona thinks.

"Anything else?"

"No. I moved right back and called you lot."

"Thank you Jess." She calls Roy over. "Constable MacGregor here will take your statement." Shona leaves them to it.

By the time she returns to the scene, the POLSA, true to his word, has a tent erected over the body. Shona is glad. She has to agree with Peter that it doesn't seem right for a nun's breasts to be open to the world.

Iain is still taking pictures when a whirlwind enters the stifling tent. Whitney, the police surgeon has arrived. "Morning troops. I knew it wouldn't be long until we met again. Still killing off the religious community of Dundee I see, Shona."

While Shona is trying to formulate a polite response, Whitney attends to her duties. She stands up and says, "Dead as the proverbial dodo, but you already knew that. See you all soon," and the whirlwind recedes.

"I'm exhausted just watching her," says Peter.

"She's certainly lively. How can she look that fresh and beautiful at five o'clock in the friggin morning? It's not fair. The rest of us look like a bag of spuds."

"Och, you look fine, Ma'am."

"A vision of beauty and radiance," says Iain.

Shona has to laugh. She can't be in a bad mood too long with this lot around. "Flattery will get you everywhere. Now, what about our dead nun? Let's get this crime scene processed and she can be removed to somewhere more private."

They all work closely together and soon have much of the evidence collected and bagged up. Iain has a beautiful cast of a partial tyre track. Someone had obviously been watering the flowers and a remnant of the water had remained in the gutter. That, and the dust had formed just the right surface for a tyre track to be left.

"Let's hope it's an unusual make. It could be our killer's vehicle," says a smiling Iain. Crime scene evidence is always guaranteed to brighten his day.

As she is leaving the gates of the church, a car drives up the street. It is stopped half way by a PC. A beautiful black woman of about forty jumps out and strolls towards Shona. She is wearing a pair of cut off shorts and a t-shirt which says 'We know what we are, but know not what we may be.' A quote from Hamlet, thinks Shona. Fairly literary then.

"Are you DI Shona McKenzie?"

"Yes."

"I'm Adanna Okafor." She shows Shona a press card.

"A reporter. You're a reporter?" Shona 's voice has risen in volume and lowered in temperature. "Get away from my crime scene."

"I know you've had problems with my colleagues in the past but…"

"Move now, or the rest of this conversation will be held in a prison cell." Shona strides past the woman.

Undeterred Okafor hurries after her. "We could work together."

Shona swivels so fast she nearly knocks the

reporter off her feet. "Are you deaf or something?" She arrives at her car, gets in, slams the door, and drives away leaving the woman in her wake.

Adanna's eyes narrow. Little does Shona know she has not heard the last from the woman. An Okafor does not give up. She saunters towards the crime scene.

Shona returns to her life of hard labour and servitude, via Costa Coffee. She orders several large cups of iced coffee to go.

"Are you having a party?" asks a far too wide awake server.

"This is to get me through the day."

"I know the feeling. Where do you work?"

"I'm a copper."

"Is your boss a bit of a tosser? You need coffee to get through the day?"

"You don't know just how right you are."

She then takes a side trip to Rough and Fraser's bakery and orders several wholemeal rolls with cold meat and salad. I could get used to this healthy lifestyle she thinks. Surely Peter must have lost some weight by now. It feels like he's been on the diet for weeks.

The team, when they return, is appreciative of the rolls. They fall on them like starving labourers.

"I bet the last supper didnae taste as good as this."

"Keeping with the ecclesiastical theme are we Peter?"

"Since this case started I cannae get churches out of my mind. I've even considered going to confession."

"That would take several months in your case," says Roy.

"Listen here buggerlugs. Keep your opinions to yourself."

"I think he's right," says Abigail. "That poor priest."

"When everyone's quite finished taking the mick out of Peter, you may want to remember we've a few murders to wrap up. Don't let me stop you having fun though. Just say when you're ready."

"Sorry, Ma'am" says Nina.

"I should jolly well think so. All this morale is killing the case. Keep your brains for thinking, not for making witty repartee." Her smile takes the sting out of the words.

"Before we start on this murder, Roy, you said you might have something on one of the dead vicars?"

"I can't be a hundred percent sure but I think I have a match."

"Go for it Roy, the floor's yours."

"I have a ninety one point three percent match on the picture of our vicar found at the Gateway, and a young man who went missing thirteen years ago." He pins both of the photos on the whiteboard. Everyone peers at them.

"I think you could be right," says Shona. "But, if he went missing that long ago how come he's turned up dead in our backyard now."

"His name at the time was Josh Guillam. He ran away from home and it looks like he changed his name to Gabriel Smith."

"Gabriel. Quite fitting considering he's probably up there with the angels as we speak," says Abigail.

"Very witty. Remind me to put you lot in for the police pantomime. So what has Josh stroke Gabriel been doing in the meantime? How did he end up in Dundee?"

"He worked as a rent boy for several years. He obviously stayed under the radar as he's never been picked up by vice. It looks like he was a bit of a drifter. He probably thought there might be some casual building work going."

“So why was he found dead dressed in a vicars costume?”

“We’d be as well conjuring up a reason from mid air. That part I have found nothing about.”

“You’ve still done well. Good work Roy. Jason, could you ring the local police in Josh’s home town. Fax through the Identikit drawing. They can go and speak to his parents. Ask them to do swabs for DNA testing to see if our corpse is their son.”

“Shall I do it now?”

“Yes, you can catch up later. Have you anything of import to tell us before you go.”

“Nothing.” He leaves the room.

“Iain, have you managed to identify the tyre track yet?”

“Not yet, but I can tell you that it belongs to a large vehicle. I’m going to do some more research. Tyres are not my forte. I’m more your bullet, blood and guts type of guy.”

“TMI, Iain. You must be a barrel of laughs when you’re out on a date.”

“I haven’t had many dates recently, Ma’am.”

“I wonder why? Go, research.”

He bounds off, full of restless energy and enthusiasm. Give Iain a puzzle to solve and he’s as happy as a monkey on cannabis.

“Nina, anything to report?”

“Searched the area from A to Z and found very little. Mostly concrete, and as per, any earth is baked hard.”

“The flower beds were watered, did that not help.”

“No. The ground was baked solid.”

“So what's with the muddy tyre track?”

“Probably a drunk having a pee in the gutter,” says Peter.

“Jeeze. I should know better than to ask a question

around here."

Shona goes to find Iain. "Did we ever come up with anything on the blood we found in St Andrews?"

"Yep. Definitely blood. We got DNA as well."

"Any hits?"

"No, but if we do have a suspect it might be enough to nail him or her."

"Any definitive on the tyre tracks?"

"The wheels are at least 19 inches. Can't pin it down to a definitive just yet. I've a mate in Aberdeen that knows more about tyres and cars. I'll give him a ring."

"Let me know the minute you've got something."

Shona hasn't been at her desk long when she is called into the Chief's office.

"Ex Lord Provost George Brown would like to know why his builders are not back at work. He says you are costing him money."

"The foreman was given the all clear yesterday, Sir. Pa Broon..." Shona takes one look at the Chief's face, "The ex Lord Provost, needs to ask his gaffer that, not me."

"You didn't think to let George Brown know that."

"I'm a police officer, Sir. Not, the ex Lord Provost's secretary."

"Don't take that tone with me. Phone George Brown, apologise, and tell him his workmen are free to return to the site."

"Yes, Sir."

She leaves the office thinking about the best way to get his body to that building site.

If that wasn't bad enough, forty minutes later she has a call from the desk sergeant.

"Ma'am, I have Stephan and Gregor Alexeyev here. They would like to talk to you."

"What do that pair of thugs want?"

"I have no idea, Ma'am. I am sure they will be delighted to share it with you."

"Bring them up."

Shona finds Peter. "I'm not speaking to the Russian twins on my own."

It didn't take Stephan long to get to the point. "You have one of my employees in your cells."

"Who might that be?"

"Mr Andrew Claypotts."

"He works for you? I don't thinks so. Claypotts, Ratray and Elgin are a family firm."

"We own half of the business."

"Well, you'll have to pretend that you own the Ratray and Elgin part. Claypotts is staying where he is."

"That is not good enough. Our business is suffering."

"Then rearrange something as he's likely to be with us for some time. Good day gentlemen." Shona stands up and walks out of the room. She'd had enough Russians in her last case and certainly doesn't want them cluttering up this one.

The next interruption is more welcome. It is the local police from Exmouth. They have news on the identity of Josh Guillam. His parents think he may be their missing son. The DNA swabs are on their way by courier. Shona hangs up the phone. It almost immediately rings. It is Mary from the mortuary.

"Shona, you might want to come across and look at your nun."

Intrigued, Shona agrees. Besides, the mortuary will be blessedly cool.

19

One look and Shona can see why Mary called her.

"That's a lot of tattoos."

"It certainly is."

The woman's left arm has a cobra winding round it, with an interesting addition. At one point it looks as though it has crawled under the skin and out again. There are also two apples, one of which is being bitten by the snake. The right arm has tattoos of several animals including a rat, bird, bat, toad and a hare. Her stomach has been transformed with the addition of a black cat. Her left leg is now a hyena and the right leg a leopard.

"A strange collection," says Shona.

"You haven't seen them all yet."

Mary and her assistant turn the dead nun over.

Shona takes in the upturned Pentagram, a symbol of occultism, which covers the whole of the dead woman's back. She says, "I feel a sudden urge to pray."

"I've been praying since she got here," says Mary.

"I think we can safely say this woman is not a nun."

"If I were a betting woman I would put a tenner on you being right."

Shona, the team, and various beverages are once more in the briefing room. The team scrutinize the photos which are now displayed on the wall. Shona notices Peter crossing himself.

"All the tattoos are in places which can be hidden,"

says Abigail. “That must mean something.”

“I agree. It's almost as though she was a nun and hiding this,” says Nina

“We got to know the nuns fairly well during our last case. They're a decent bunch. I don't think our dead woman is anything to do with the Catholic Church.” Shona doesn’t know where this case is going but her gut instinct tells her that this is true.

“Ma'am, I dinnae think the Catholic Church would let anyone with those tattoos inside their doors,” says Peter. Being Catholic, Peter is the go to guy for anything RC related.

“So, why is a dead woman, who would appear to be a witch, dressed in nun's clothes?”

“Not a clue, but it's our job to find out. We also need to find out the identities of our victims, and what they have in common. Peter, you're coming with me to visit a few churches, the rest of you get searching and see if you can come up with anything.”

They are no sooner out the door than Peter says, “Can we go and visit St Ninian's first?”

“Okay, but why.”

Peter looks sheepish. “The wife's signed me up for Slimming World. I've to get weighed. There's a class there today.”

“As we're visiting churches anyway I don't see why not. We'll start there.”

After visiting St Ninian's they are no further forwards in the investigation, but Peter is grinning ear to ear.

“The lassie that runs the group, Fiona, says I've lost twelve pounds.”

“Twelve pounds? Despite moaning you've been eating like a horse.”

“Aye. The wife will be pleased. I'm going to text

her."

"I'm surprised you even know how to text."

"My daughter taught me. She says I need to come into the twenty first century."

"She's a wise girl your daughter."

They continue the rounds of the Dundee Churches, meeting some lovely people in the process, but getting no hits on their victims. There is some sort of gathering on in the town. It is packed. Someone approaches them and hands them a leaflet about saving their souls. The Muslims and Buddhists also have a go to gain their allegiance.

"Dundee, seems to be awash with churches and religious communities. For a city where crime is rife I'm surprised," says Shona

"The folks o' Dundee are a lovely bunch on the whole. We just meet the bad ones."

The team has come up with nothing either, so Shona calls a press conference for later in the day. She wants to get the word out about the latest victims to see if anyone recognises them. Surely someone must be missing their loved ones, she thinks. How sad that anyone can die without a soul marking his or her passing.

She widens the press conference to a hundred mile radius. She also invites the Scottish Editions of *The Times, The Guardian* etc. Surely that will ring a bell with someone.

Double Eckie once again works his magic, leaving Shona with some top notch images for the press. The man could have painted the ceiling of the Sistine Chapel and done a better job than Michelangelo. The Chief says that Shona can handle the press conference. His actual words were, "Since you arrived I spend more time with the press than I have in the rest of my career.

You sort it." Two hours later, at a time when most people are eating their tea, Shona is in front of the Nation's media. STV have also got wind of it and have turned up. All to the good thinks Shona. More exposure means more chance of identifying the victims.

"Police Scotland can confirm that the bodies of four unidentified victims have been found in Dundee over the past two weeks. Their pictures are on the screen behind me. The press have also been issued with these pictures. If you have any information pertaining to these victims or these crimes then please contact Detective Inspector Shona McKenzie, the senior investigating officer on 0300 572 8761."

Shona quickly shields her eyes against what feels like a million watt barrage of flashlight. They are accompanied by questions

"Troy Severs, *STV*. Do you think these murders are connected?"

"Without more evidence it is difficult to say."

"Adanna Okafor, *The Courier*, is it true that all the victims are members of the Christian community?"

"That is part of our ongoing investigation. We cannot discuss it at this time." I'm going to kill her, thinks Shona.

"Sarah Monkton, *Press and Journal*. Why do you think there are so many serial killer's in Dundee?"

"I don't know, but it would be helpful if they would move to Aberdeen."

The reporters laugh. I wasn't being funny, thinks Shona.

The reporters disperse, but one remains. She not only remains but comes after Shona.

"Ms Okafor, why are you following me? This is a restricted area."

"Spare me a few minutes of your time for a chat. I don't want us to be at odds."

"We have nothing to say to each other outside of a press conference."

"I know you've had problems with my colleagues in the past. I want to change that. It could be to both our advantages."

For some peculiar reason, Shona caves. "Come with me. You've got five minutes." She hurries off. Adanna's long stride easily keeps up with her.

"Spit it out," says Shona, once they are seated in her office.

"I know working with some of my colleagues has been difficult for you."

"Difficult! That's an understatement."

Adanna is unperturbed by Shona's tone. "Okay, impossible. They've used every trick they can to get a good story, even if it interferes with what you're doing. I'd say reporters are down there with Satan in your eyes."

"That's more like it." Shona's voice has lowered slightly.

"I would like to change that. We should work together. We can report the truth, and only what you give me permission to report. I've got a first class honours degree from Oxford. I can make anything dramatic without veering from the truth."

Shona's jaw drops. Her brain is so scrambled she takes a few seconds to formulate the right words. "Are you telling me you're wanting to help us?"

"I am. You have my word."

"What's in it for you?"

"When your case is resolved I get the first scoop on the details. No holding back."

"I'll have to think about it. Give me your card."

The reporter drops her business card on Shona's desk and then holds out her hand. They shake, and the woman leaves.

Peter is even more stunned than Shona. If that were possible. “You're going into league with a reporter? Did I actually hear that right?”

“You did. She seems fairly sensible and genuinely helpful.”

“I never in a million years saw that coming. Ma'am, you never cease to amaze me.”

“This time I’ve even managed to amaze myself. Hobnobbing with journalists would be the last thing on my bucket list.”

“The results of this little liaison could be interesting, Ma’am. I can’t wait to see them.”

“Watch this space. It’s knocking off time. Send everyone home. Hopefully the morning's gaudy headlines will have the phone ringing off the hook.”

Shona goes home via the Chinese. As it's Easter, Douglas has taken the kids away to a caravan in the Lake District for a week so she's home alone. She orders salt and pepper squid, chicken in yellow bean sauce, special fried rice and an extra large portion of prawn crackers. The crackers are for Shakespeare. As she suspected the cat is waiting for her when she reaches the door. Shakespeare's highly developed nose can smell a prawn cracker a mile out. Shona isn't sure who enjoys their meal more. She pulls out her mobile to try and ring Douglas. No go. He’s obviously out of range.

20

The next morning's headlines are fairly mild. Adanna, true to her word, has reported everything correctly but with a strong dash of drama. It is almost inspired.
The headline reads:

"Four Deaths: One Killer?"

> 'Dundee police are on a search for the identities of four recent murder victims. The question everyone is asking, are these people linked by blood or circumstance? This cannot be answered, as the Police do not, as yet, know the identities of the deceased. Detective Inspector Shona McKenzie is asking for members of the public to help with this puzzle. Do you know any of these people? If so, you could be instrumental in solving a mystery and catching a killer.'

It continues like this for a few more paragraphs, and finishes with:

> 'Are you the one person in Dundee who can assist the police? Step forward and take your place in the annals of Dundee history. The police need you.'

"She's good, isn't she, Ma'am?" says Peter.

"Even I'm impressed. Maybe she's not so bad after

all. I'm off to grab a coffee before the onslaught of calls."

Shona barely has time to put her backside on her leather chair, never mind take a sip of her liquid restorative, when the phone rings.

"Duty Sergeant, Ma'am. I've a woman standing here who says she has information for you."

"That was quick. Send her up."

A woman, who looks like she's been battered by life and circumstance, takes the offered chair.

"How can I help you Mrs...?"

"Bellamy. Mrs Bellamy." The woman stops.

Shona says gently, "You have some information for me?"

"My wean, Morag, was taken when she was two. I've never seen her since. The woman in the paper looks just like my other lassie, Mhairi."

"Do you have a photo we can compare, Mrs Bellamy?"

The woman pulls out a snapshot of a young woman. There is some resemblance to the dead woman, although the woman in the photo looks much softer.

"There is a similarity. Is Mhairi still living around here?"

"Aye, she is."

"Could you ask her to come in and see us? We will need to take swabs to see if our woman and your daughter are related. Would you be willing to give us swabs as well?"

"Aye." The downtrodden woman looks resigned.

Shona escorts her to a waiting room. Once Iain arrives the swabs are quickly taken. The woman leaves, assuring Shona that her daughter will be in shortly.

"I'm not sure whether I want it to be her daughter or not," says Iain.

"It would be a bit of a mixed blessing."

Shona still hasn't managed to get through her coffee when the phone rings again. The man at the other end says he knows the woman.

"Thanks for getting in touch. Can I have more details?" She grabs a pen from the holder on her desk.

"Her name is Penny Smith-Lanson. We run a drop-in at our church where we serve soup and pudding. She's homeless so she comes for a feed."

"What church are you at?"

"St Xystus. We're in Kirkton."

"Do you know anything else about her?"
"Not much. She had a posh English accent. I'll ask around and see if I can find out anything."

"Thanks. Let me know immediately you have anything more."

So two hits on the woman, both with different names. Maybe we'll solve two mysteries at once, thinks Shona. That would be a good day.

She briefs the team.

"Maybe they're all homeless," says Nina.

"Possibly, but why has no one else come forward."

"Many of the folks who use the drop-ins are on the fringes. They wouldn't want to talk to the police," says Roy.

"Anybody got any idea how many drop-ins there are in Dundee?"

"There are wee booklets somewhere. Uniform give them out to anyone who's begging."

"Right, I'm going to find Brian Gevers. He might have some notion, or at least find me the relevant booklet."

Brian has never seen any of the victims before, but he does ferret out a couple of leaflets. "Do you need any help, Ma'am?"

"I don't at the moment, Brian. Unless you know where Auld Jock is?" Auld Jock is a local tramp. He's a Dundee institution and the whole city tends to look after him.

"I haven't seen him all summer, Ma'am."

"Neither have we, so I'm a bit worried."

"I'll see what I can do, Ma'am. Everyone likes Jock so I'm sure they'll be willing to keep a look out."

"You're a gem, Brian. I owe you one."

"Just keep me in mind if a spot opens up in CID."

"The first spot is yours."

After a quick look at the leaflets they are no further forward. The drop-ins all happen on different days and different times.

"Ring round the churches and ask for the contact details for the head volunteers. We'll get them to come in to look at the photos. It'll be quicker than visiting. Roy, you get the numbers and we'll do the ringing."

An hour later they are waiting for several volunteers to arrive. They were reliably informed that two of them are currently in Lanzarote with their kids. Four others are going to come in when they finish work.

"Could we go and get something to eat? I'm starving as we've no' had lunch."

"There's nothing in the canteen you can eat. Its nickname isn't stodge city without a reason."

"Doreen said she would whip me up a slimming world omelette any time."

"Go on then, but you'd better be quick." The team is out the door before she gets the second part out.

They needn't have worried about their timing. It took what seemed like forever for the volunteers to arrive. The general complaint seemed to be that the Kingsway was a car park both ways. Hardly a car was moving. They managed to interview them quickly and with no results. One of the volunteers thought he recognised the man found on the steps of Kings.

"I think he came in a couple of times about six months ago."

"Do you know his name?"

"I can't remember. We get so many people through the doors."

"Thanks. If it should come back to you, contact us straight away."

"I will."

No stone left unturned and yet still nowhere near finding out the identity of their victims.

"Roy, see what you can find on a Penny Smith-Lanson. I think that's who our woman is. Nina, do a search on HOLMES for her name. There might be a missing persons report on her, somewhere in England."

Twenty minutes later she has her answer. A missing person report had been filed for a Penny Smith-Lanson. She has been missing for four years and hails from Berkshire. From the photos their tattooed woman and the missing Penny are one and the same. They would still need DNA to be sure. However, given that Penny could also be Morag Bellamy it isn't that straightforward.

"What a beggars muddle," says Shona.

"I couldn't have put it better myself," says Nina. "How do we handle this?"

"We wait for the DNA results to come back on Mrs Bellamy and Mhairi. If it's a match with our corpse then we work with the police in Berkshire to get the couple who brought Penny up transferred here for questioning."

"That could be days. What if Penny's parents get

wind of this in the meantime?"

"We'll have to take that chance. They could have been involved in trafficking. That's the important point."

"Okay."

"Given that one of our victims is from England, I think we need to widen the search. Send the identikits to every division in Police Scotland. Jason can help you."

The photos having been sent out, they are now playing a waiting game. Shona has no clue where to go next with this. Why would anyone be killing and dressing their victims up as religious figures? This makes even less sense than her previous cases. She decides to do a search for any similar cases. The nearest she can get is John Wayne Gacy in America. Gacy was a bisexual who did good works at charitable institutions by dressing as a clown. This earned him the name of the clown killer. He stabbed, asphyxiated or strangled thirty-three young men, after luring them to his home. He had worked as a morgue attendant and had trained in embalming techniques.

Were there enough similarities to make it a copycat, she thinks. She goes to run it past the team.

"I widnae think so," says Peter. "It's no just men who are being attacked. We've a woman. Gacy only attacked men."

"If it wasn't for the cross, I would say we have two killers on our hands. Gacy didn't desecrate his victims either, or embalm them."

"He was a trained embalmer though," says Abigail.

"Have we looked into the mortuary attendants?" Nina raises a valid point.

"I didn't really want to go down that route. The thought of any of Mary's staff doing this makes me sick."

"It's no' a cheery thought, Ma'am."

"Do you think the cross could be a spin on the clown costume Gacy wore when he killed his victims?" asks Nina.

"He did what?" Roy's voice had risen so much it could crack glass. "Did you say he wore a clown suit?"

"It was some sort of perverted logic which only he could understand. Maybe he thought it would be better for them to be killed by a clown. It was probably a weird sexual fantasy." Shona stands up, "I'm off to speak to Mary. This is something which needs to be done face to face."

"I dinnae envy you that job."

On that cheery note Shona heads for her air conditioned car. Be thankful for the little things she thinks.

Mary's office isn't air conditioned but she leaves the door open from the mortuary. Shona sinks into a comfortable chair and sighs. "Can I move here until the heatwave is over?"

"Feel free. It would be nice to have you around."

"You might not be saying that in a minute."

"So what's got you rattled then, Shona. You're not your usual witty self."

"Before we discuss it, can I ask you if you know how our victims died?"

"In graphic detail?"

"Maybe just the edited highlights. I've enough graphic detail in this case already."

"The chap from the Gateway had opiate poisoning. His organs were stuffed full of them. With the levels I'd say they were injected. Unless he wanted to kill himself and swallowed hundreds of codeine pills. Unlikely given the way he was found."

"So someone injected him with opiate, embalmed him, and completed the process with a cross?"

"That's about right. Strange even by your standards."

"I need to ask something," says Shona, her voice low.

"I take it that's what's getting you down?"

"It is. I'm sorry I have to ask this, but could any of your assistants be my perpetrator?"

Mary doesn't even skip a heartbeat. "No. No way."

"Are you sure Mary? Whoever did this has been trained. Are any of your staff acting any differently?"

"No. I know them too well, Shona. There's no way they could have turned their hand to this. I'd be willing to stake my life on it."

"You do know I am going to have to investigate them don't you?" She pauses and says softly, "And you."

Mary just looks sad. This is by far the hardest conversation Shona has had in her career.

"I'm sorry Mary."

"I know you are, Shona. I know you have to do your job."

"Do you mind if we start today?"

"No. Would you like me to get my guys in so you can explain?"

"Please. I'll get my whole team in so we can get it done more quickly."

The interviews go speedily and it is apparent everyone is accounted for and has an alibi for the times in question. They all seem above board and professional in their approach. Everyone that is, except one young trainee who is obviously hiding something.

"Where were you on the nights of..." Shona rattles of the dates.

"Why do you want to know?"

"I ask the questions. It's not a difficult one. Where were you?"

"I don't have to tell you."

"That's right you don't. However, you're giving me the impression you have something to hide. So it will be better for you if you tell us."

"I'd rather not."

"I've had enough of this. You're coming with us to the station."

"You can't arrest me. What for?"

"Perverting the course of justice."

"What? How am I doing that?"

"By refusing to tell us where you were."

He thinks for a few seconds, then, "Okay. I was out with mates."

"Which mates and where? Can they vouch for you?"

"If I tell you what I was doing will you believe me and leave my mates out of it?"

"It depends on what your next sentence is. It also depends on how fast you tell me. I'm losing patience."

"I was out Dogging."

"Dogging? There's a dogging scene in Dundee?"

Peter chips in, "It died out around here a few years ago. It's a bit suspicious that it's reared its ugly head just in time to provide you with an alibi."

"Why would I tell you that if it wasn't true. I'm not exactly going to be broadcasting the scene to the police, am I?"

"Don't be so cheeky sonny boy. Keep a civil tongue in your head."

Shona steps in, "Give me the name and number of someone who can confirm your alibi. Sergeant Johnston, keep him here until I get back."

The alibi pans out. "You're free to go. I'm passing

your hobby on to uniform. They're going to be over it like bees around nectar. Tell your pals the dogging scene is over. If I discover even a whisper of it I'm arresting you. I'm also going to tell your boss. She might not want someone who does that as a hobby, on her training programme."

Shona is right. Mary is not amused. "I can't exactly kick him off the programme but I'm going to be watching him like a hawk. He'd better treat these bodies with respect and decorum otherwise he will be reevaluating his career choice."

"That's the spirit, Mary. You'll be glad to know everyone else checked out. They're a fine upstanding bunch. Not that I was expecting anything less from anyone working with you. They always strike me as being professional to the core."

"Thanks, Shona. Although I can't believe I'm thanking you. Now if you'll excuse me I have customers waiting." It is apparent that Mary will be working late into the night to catch up. She is as dedicated to the search for truth as Shona, and much of her day has been wasted whilst she and her staff were being interviewed.

Shona dismisses the team and says they are free to return to their loved ones. "We can update HOLMES in the morning."

Surprised at the early let off the team are out the door before she can finish her sentence.

Tonight it is curry for one, shorts, t-shirt, a DVD and a glass of Talisker whisky. It makes a change for Shona. During a murder investigation she usually works gruelling hours. Relaxing doesn't usually feature.

21

The next player gazes at the body before him. He knows that he has to work quickly. A slight glance; the trolley contains everything he needs. He takes in the instruments, glinting in the sunlight. The room is spotless, as is the naked body. He steps forward and picks up a large, green bottle of antiseptic. The top is unscrewed and a little fluid poured onto the first swab. The top is screwed on tight and the bottle returned to precisely the spot it came from.

Next the body is massaged. Firm strokes. Loosening limbs and muscles. Preparing the body for the free flow of fluid. Every stroke is deliberate, precise, in just the right place. Perfection is needed. The process smooth, he feels for the optimum relaxation. Once it is reached he steps back.

He deftly prepares the machine pouring in the fluid. He plugs it in. It is now prepared and ready for him to flip the switch at the appropriate time.

He picks up the scalpel, the handle fitting his hand perfectly. For a moment it is held just above the skin, and then the perfect cut is made. Swab the blood and a surgical tie is expertly applied. The drain tube is slipped into the vein and the tie tightened. The manoeuvre is repeated on the artery using a cannula. The blood is cleaned away and the man bends over. The switch is flicked, a rhythmic thrumming and the fluid slowly enters the body.

The limbs are massaged to keep the fluid moving. The machine completes its efficient replacement of the blood. The trochar is used to clean the organs and cavities.

The body is now ready for the next part of the process.

22

The following morning finds Shona running along the promenade at Broughty Ferry listening to Katie Melua. The music and the merest hint of a sea breeze keep her moving one foot in front of the other, whilst the heat urges her to stop. Her long legs are graceful in motion. She is dazzled by the sunlight bouncing off the cerulean blue of the Tay Estuary. Something moves in the water. She stops, breathing in the tangy scent of the salt sea air. A shoal of dolphins surfaces and performs a joyous dance in the sunlight before diving again. This truly is a beautiful part of the world, she thinks. She is thankful she has moved back here despite the circumstances surrounding the move. Her ex-husband walked out on her the minute they arrived. It was worth it just for today. The run invigorates her and clears her head of thoughts of murder. By the time she drives to work she is singing along to Katie.

"Morning troops. How are we all this fine morning?" She dispenses a stunning smile and packets of chocolate biscuits. "None for you, Peter. Don't undo your good work."

"What's got you in such a good mood? I'm allowed a Kit Kat." He unwraps and bites into one before Shona can object.

"It's a beautiful day and we haven't been called out to a murder scene. What's not to like? Have any of the other divisions got back about our John Does?"

"All we've had time to do is make tea and coffee,"

says Jason.

"Get your priorities right why don't you? Hop to it. I'm off to check my emails and answer machine." She grabs a few biscuits in case she starves to death before lunch.

There is nothing on either so she resorts to eating the biscuits while she thinks. She's wondering if the homeless angle is significant. The first victim might well have been homeless. He looked and smelt like he hadn't had a wash in a while. The others were clean as a whistle though. The way they were dressed obviously means something but what? The tattoos seemed to be pointing towards a satanic element. But why would worshippers of Satan kill one of their own?

The ring of a phone startles her out of her thoughts.

"It's Dan Bertram here, the DI from Inverness."

"Hi Dan. What can I do for you?"

"It's more what I can do for you. I think we have a hit on one of your unidentified bodies."

"Shoot."

"The scruffy looking bloke could be Kieran O'Shaughnessy. He was a drifter who found his way here from Ireland. No one paid much attention when he disappeared. The folk who run the homeless shelter are used to their service users coming and going."

"Have you anything else for me to go on?"

"Nothing. I've got the number of the shelter. Might be worth giving them a ring."

She takes it down. "Thanks Dan."

She dials the number and is soon through to the supervisor of the hostel.

"I haven't really got much I can give you. Kieran would appear every few nights looking for a bed and some food. He kept to himself. I think he came from Cork."

"The county or the city?"

"No idea I'm afraid. Is he okay?"

"We're not sure. We'll let the local police know if we find anything out."

She rings Cork and tells them she'll send the details through. They're happy to investigate it further.

"That's two out of four victims who were homeless," says Peter, once she has briefed the others.

"I think the homeless angle is the most likely, "says Shona. "All we need to do is find out why the homeless are being killed, branded and dumped in Dundee."

"Nothing much to worry about then," says Nina.

"Not a thing. Should be a breeze. Why are my cases always off the planet, never mind the wall?"

"I'd say they're out of our universe altogether," says Abigail. "We never had this much fun in Skye."

"Fun! That's not exactly what I'd call it. More like slow torture."

The next phone call shoves all thoughts of dead vicars out of their heads.

"Ma'am, there's been an explosion up at Camperdown Park," says the Desk Sergeant. "They've asked you to attend."

"An explosion? Where? Is it the restaurant?"

"Not sure Ma'am, but uniform are up there and so are the medics. They'll direct you."

Shona hurries to the team office. "Grab stab vests and guns. Emergency in Camperdown. I'll arrange for us to be blue-lighted."

The urgency in her tone galvanises them and they move as a man without question.

When they arrive, there's a large crowd standing outside. The whole area has been declared a crime scene. Some of the swarm are remonstrating with the police on duty.

"My car's in there. How am I meant tae get the bairns home?"

"I paid to get into that zoo and then you lot drag me out."

The Constables remain calm but the look in their eyes says they'd like to add several more bodies to the overall count. If there are any. Shona is fervently hoping there are not.

"The less shouting you do the quicker we can get on with our job," says Shona. "Stop harassing the constables. I'm in charge here and what I say goes. Now take your kids home on the bus and leave this area."

A few look belligerent.

She steps forward, looks them straight in the eye and says, "Now."

The hangers on decide it might be a good idea to comply.

Camperdown is a huge park, with acres of ground, much of which is forested. Many years ago it was the estate of the Earl of Camperdown. It has an imposing house, duck ponds, stables, and a small zoo which has a cafe. However, none of these are the scene of the explosion. Several teenage boys had been taking advantage of the Easter break and the glorious weather to explore the park. They had come across an abandoned outbuilding at the far fringes of the park. It is this building which has exploded.

Shona takes in the scene. The fire brigade are dealing with a blaze which has taken hold in the trees. They are also busy moving rubble assisted by uniform. There are several ambulances and the crew are working feverishly on a number of boys who don't look like they are going to make it.

"What's the story?" Shona asks the POLSA.

"We're not sure if the bomb was deliberately set or if it's anything to do with the boys."

"I'm sure the boys wouldn't try to blow themselves up. If they're bright enough to get a bomb together then surely they'd be bright enough to get out of the way?"

"You're probably right but I've learned enough in this job to realise you should never underestimate the utter stupidity of a teenage boy. Especially when they're trying to look cool in front of their mates."

"Has anybody checked the area for secondary devices?"

"No. We wanted to see if there were any survivors. We thought it was worth the risk."

Shona takes charge. "Everyone back. Apart from the firefighters that is. Wait for the army bomb disposal team."

"My paramedics are staying where they are." At five foot ten inches, Shona has to strain to look up at the beanpole in front of her.

"Your paramedics could die if another bomb goes off. Surely you can move the casualties back a bit?"

"Not 'til they're stable. They could die if we move them."

Implacable meets immovable.

"This is my crime scene and I say move them."

"This is my disaster area and they stay."

"Don't they teach you to preserve your own life first?"

Implacable just stares at her, unblinking.

It becomes a moot point. Two of the boys are declared dead. The others are carted off in ambulances, and implacable jumps in to one of them.

Several firefighters and all the uniform have moved

to a safer distance. The blaze is brought under control and the trees around the area are being sprayed with water.

"Ma'am, this young woman would like to talk to you." A Constable beckons the woman forward. She is wearing a Camperdown Park Wildlife Centre T-shirt.

"We're worried about the bears. They're on the rampage. We're waiting for the vet to come and tranquilize them."

"As if things aren't bad enough. Now we've to worry about bears escaping. Thanks for letting me know." She walks over to the POLSA.

"Do we have an identity for any of the boys?"

"No, Ma'am. We couldn't even search for phones as the paramedics were working on them."

"That's one of my first priorities, once I'm sure the area is safe."

She sees Adanna and a photographer from *The Courier* approaching. Given that the reporter has been fairly amicable so far Shona bites back her usual sharp response.

"Stay back. This is not just a crime scene but could blow up any minute. How did you get in here anyway?"

"I know a back way in where the wall has broken down. We won't get in your way," says Adanna, "but can we interview you?"

"What here gives you the impression I've time for an interview? I'm in the middle of a major incident."

"When you do have time. I honestly want to work with you, not against you."

Shona is still suspicious but gives the woman the benefit of the doubt. "Wait over there." Shona points to a clearing well beyond the crime scene. "I'll come and find you." Much to Shona's surprise they do as they are asked. The photographer takes out a telephoto lens and starts to take pictures.

"I want to see those photos before they hit the headlines," she shouts over to them.

Adanna grins, "Whatever you say goes."

"They seem awfy amenable, Ma'am," says Peter.

"I agree, they are awfully amenable. I'm sure she's up to..." She stops short. "Oi you pair. Where are you going?"

Roy and Jason are heading towards the rubble.

"I thought I saw movement behind the rubble," says Roy, the urgency in his voice apparent. "We're going to check."

"You can't go over there. It could explode any minute."

Both the young coppers ignore her and continue on their path. They reach the explosion site and disappear behind the stones. "There's someone here," shouts Jason.

"Phone an ambulance," Shona shouts over her shoulder as, throwing caution to the wind, she hurries towards them.

Most of the team are now helping move rubble from an injured teenager, only a small part of a hand is showing. It was a slight movement of this that had alerted eagle eyed Roy. When they get the unconscious teen out they realise it's a girl.

"Get the firefighters. They'll have a board to move her on." Abigail complies and the firefighters take over. The ambulance, the Army bomb disposal unit, and the team to remove the dead boys, all arrive at the same time.

"Shona. I didn't think I'd be seeing you again," says the Major in charge. "We seem to get a lot of call outs to Dundee since you took over." Despite the jocularity he is efficiently commanding his men and they take over the area.

It's time for Shona to have a word with the press

who are still waiting patiently. She gives them a brief overview of the situation and gives the go ahead for the photos. All seems to be above board. Adanna and her sidekick rush off to get it in that evening's *Telegraph.*

There isn't any more they can do in the way of collecting evidence. As she is leaving the site she hears the drone of a helicopter. Someone has obviously contacted the BBC. "Vultures, the whole damn lot of them," she says to Nina. Nina, wisely remains silent.

She is leaving the park when a couple of terrified looking women run up to her.

"My boy was in there. Oliver Lawrence. Have you seen him?"

"My son, Jack, was there with him."

"I'm afraid we don't know anything. There have been some casualties who have been taken to Ninewells Hospital. Come with me."

The Accident and Emergency department is packed. Shona takes the mothers over to reception and flashes her ID card. She and the ladies are taken through to the treatment area. Mrs Lawrence identifies her son, who is currently on a ventilator and hooked up to a number of machines. Jack is nowhere to be seen.

Shona is gentle, "I am sorry to have to tell you that there were two deaths."

Jack's mother goes white and crumples to the ground.

"Can I have some help here," Shona shouts to a passing nurse.

The woman is soon lying on a trolley and her cheeks have the merest hint of colour. "Mrs...?"

"McCutcheon. Molly McCutcheon."

"Mrs McCutcheon. What does Jack look like and what was he wearing today?"

"He's tall for his age. Five foot six, wi' ginger hair. He won't comb it so it's always a mess. I think he was wearing a Celtic football shirt and cut off jeans. He disnae wear anything else."

Shona, with a limited knowledge of football is at a bit of a loss here. "What colour shirt would that be?"

The woman, even in shock, looks at Shona like she's a sausage short of a cooked breakfast. "Green. Why are you asking me that, when my laddie might be dead?"

Shona casts her brain back over the disaster area. She can't remember seeing any green shirts. "The nurses will look after you and I'll be back in a few minutes. Shona wanders up the corridor and pulls out her phone.

"Mary, it's Shona. Have you got the boys from Camperdown Park yet?"

"I do. What a dreadful situation."

Shona gives the description of the missing Jack.

"Neither of them fit that description. One of them has dark hair, and the other one is Chinese."

This still doesn't help Shona as Jack might still be under the rubble. She returns to Mrs. McCutcheon's bedside. "We don't know where your son is Molly. He isn't one of those who have been found dead so far."

Molly still looks like she'd cave at a strong breath. Shona also has several other boys to identify. She needn't have worried about that. Peter and Abigail arrive with several sets of anxious looking parents. It takes them a couple of hours to identify all the boys, including the ones who are up at the morgue. In the meantime Jack has phoned his mother. He'd gone off with his girlfriend for the day and left his pals to it. One ray of sunshine in an otherwise miserable day.

"I didn't even know he had a girlfriend," says his mother. "Wait till I get hold of him."

Shona is sure that the most that will become of Jack is that he will be hugged to death.

"Do we know what happened yet?" asks Nina, when they return to the office.

"I haven't heard. The Army and the fire services are on it. I'm hoping to get an update soon. In the meantime there's a ton of paperwork to be done." Then she adds, "Good work today team. Roy well done on spotting that girl."

Roy doesn't respond but he stands a little taller. It's unusual for him to be getting compliments from the boss. She is usually bollocking him.

An hour later they still haven't heard, so Shona sends everyone home. She is just leaving when the phone rings.

"DI McKenzie."

The news she is given stuns her. She hangs up and drives home thinking about the call, wondering if there was anything she could have done to prevent the explosion.

23

The team is, for once, lost for words. Eventually Nina breaks the silence.

"Did you say the explosives came from the Army?"

Shona looks at her without talking. She eventually says, "Yes."

"How?" asks Peter.

"Surely it can't be..." He doesn't even want to say the name.

"No. As you know that's impossible. Not directly anyway."

Abigail's head is moving from side to side as she follows the conversation. Her brows are puckered. "What are you all talking about."

Roy opens his mouth to reply but Shona steps in. "I think the explosives were left behind from one of our previous cases."

"You mean you've had a case like this before."

"Not quite. Someone tried to blow up Myercroft Academy a few years ago. No deaths though. That outbuilding was probably where excess explosives were stored."

Silence falls. Then Peter says, "The Chief's going to have a floopy when he hears."

"Good Scottish word, Peter. However, given the circumstances it may not fully cover what the Chief is going to say."

Shona is right. The Chief is not only unimpressed but

white hot with anger.

"Inspector, why were these explosives not found at the resolution of your previous case?"

"We did do a search, Sir, but that outbuilding would have been completely hidden by trees and undergrowth. You would barely have been able to see it."

"That is no excuse. Children have died. There will have to be an investigation into this."

"Sir, I feel sick at the thought of those children, but we did everything we could. Sniffer dogs even went in and didn't find any explosives in the park."

"Usually you would be suspended whilst this investigation takes place. However, given that you are in the middle of a high profile case you can remain in your post."

"Thank you, Sir."

For once, Shona means it. She thought she might be relieved of her duties.

Despite feeling like the sword of Damocles is about to fall she has to pull herself together. With a case to solve and a team to lead she doesn't have time to fall apart. She has the urge for chocolate and goes to the canteen. She leaves with several bars and heads to her office, thinking of shutting herself in and eating it all. Common sense and compassion kick in and she shares it around.

"Did we ever get round to sending the details of Kieran O'Shaughnessy through to Cork?" The blank looks are her answer. "Jason, go and do it now.

Jason does her bidding and she says to the others. "This homeless angle is bothering me. Especially since no one has seen auld Jock for a few weeks. I'm concerned about him."

"Jock often does walkabout when the weather's

nice, Ma'am. He's probably off somewhere else for a wee walking holiday."

"I'm still worried. Send his picture out to the whole of Police Scotland. Tell them we're just concerned for his safety and to let us know if they've seen him."

"Righty ho, Ma'am. Best to check. Roy can we trust you to dae that without mucking it up?"

"I'm sure I can cope. It's not exactly rocket science."

"I'm never sure where you're concerned laddie."

"Has anyone got a picture of Jock?" asks Roy.

"I've got some," says Iain. "I was practicing with the new camera and Jock was in for a feed. Him and Maggie did a spot of posing for me."

"Only you, Iain, could turn an old tramp into a film star."

"They're good shots, Ma'am."

"I'm sure they're thrilling. You send them as you've got them already. Abigail you come with me. We're going to tote the identikits of the two remaining victims around any drop-ins that are on today."

"Are you pair off for a free feed while we sit here starving and working our fingers to the bone?" asks Peter.

"Don't be so dramatic, Peter. The most we'll get is a bowl of soup or a toasty. It's not exactly Egon Ronay standard in these places."

"It's still food."

Shona and Abigail leave him to moan. They decide to walk into town to visit the Steeple first. The sun is beating down and it is a pleasure to be out of the office. This is despite the fact that the most picturesque sight they see is a building site. Dundee is in the middle of a regeneration phase and this involves a lot of rebuilding.

The vicar at the Steeple welcomes them and agrees they can show the photos around. It's a wasted effort.

They walk up to the Friary and repeat the process. Again, no positive response. No one knows the dead men. All they have to show for the day is a suntan, and a full stomach. They were, as Peter thought, offered food.

By the time she gets back, Cork have been in touch. The dead vicar is Kieran O'Shaughnessy. He had gone missing a couple of years ago, leaving behind a wife and three kids. A victim of the banking crisis, he lost his job in a bank which led to him having some sort of breakdown. He walked out the door one day to buy eggs, and never returned.

Shona dials the number for the police station in Cork. She is soon put through to the senior investigating officer.

"Colm, it's Shona McKenzie here from Dundee. Thanks for pinning down the identity of our victim."

"Us Garda are always willing to help a fellow officer. Though it's sad, we're glad Mrs O'Shaungnessy has found her husband."

"We'll need to confirm it for sure. Could you collect DNA from his children and get it sent through?"

"It'll be on its way within the hour."

She is sitting contemplating a cold cup of coffee when Iain knocks on her door, and bounds in.

"Come in why don't you."

"The DNA results are in on Penny Smith-Lanson. It turns out she really is Morag Bellamy."

"That poor woman. She lost her daughter and is then going to find and lose her again in one day. What a mare this is going to be."

"When we release the body who on earth do we release it to?" asks Iain.

"It will be while before this body is released. In the meantime I'm going to get the Berkshire police involved to arrest the Smith-Lansones. Their day isn't exactly going to play out as the planned."

"It's certainly interesting working with you, Ma'am."

Shona and Nina step out of the car in front of a beautifully maintained garden. Despite the heat and the threat of drought restrictions the garden is a riot of colour. Hanging baskets, bursting with flowers, are arranged on each side of a neatly painted door. They knock but there is no answer.

"I think I can hear someone inside," says Nina. "Might be better to knock harder."

Shona gives the letterbox a vigorous rattle. Mrs Bellamy comes to the door in a dressing gown, holding a hairdryer. The minute she sees Shona, fear clouds her eyes.

"Come in." She moves back and says, "I'll put some clothes on."

"Mrs Bellamy. Is there anyone with you?"

"Mhairi's just nipped to the shops. She'll be back in a minute."

"We'll wait until she returns."

"I'll put some clothes on."

By the time she has dressed, Mhairi has returned carrying two pints of milk and a packet of bacon.

Shona gives the young woman time to deposit the groceries and sit down.

"We have evidence which confirms that the girl in the picture is your daughter."

Mrs Bellamy and Mhairi look hopeful. Then the resigned look reappears. It's as if the woman knows that this is not good news.

"I'm sorry to have to tell you that she is dead."

The woman just sits there as though frozen. Her daughter puts her arm round her and draws her close.

"Can I see her?"

"At the moment you can't. We need to investigate the circumstances of her disappearance first. You should be able to see her soon."

"Do you think she came back to Dundee to look for her real family?"

"I would think she did, Mrs Bellamy."

They take their leave.

"Do you really think that young lass came to find her long lost relatives?"

"It's possible but not probable. It was probably a quirk of fate that brought her here. I wasn't going to say that to that poor woman though. She needs a little bit of hope to cling to."

"You're as soft as butter really, Shona."

"Don't go spreading rumours like that. Anarchy will erupt."

On the way back in the car Shona catches up on Nina's love life. Nina seems to have a different man in her life every few weeks. She can't remember who the last one was and what he did. There was a Kyle and an Andros but they seem to be long gone. This one seems to be called Allesandro and he's Italian.

"He's got dreamy eyes and an accent to die for," says Nina.

"Any other pertinent details?"

"He's a doctor and drives a Jag. It's a convertible."

"I knew there had to be more to it than dreamy eyes. I suppose a boyfriend with a convertible is a real asset in weather like this."

"Shona, I'm shocked. How could you think I would be so mercenary?" Her laughter belies her words.

"I know you too well, Nina Chakrabarti."

The inane chatter is a welcome break from the intensity of the case.

On her return to the office she realises her break is over. The Duty sergeant is waiting for her. That never bodes well.

"Body found in a wee church in Glenesk. From the description it matches your case."

"Where's Glenesk?"

"Up past Edzell."

Shona is none the wiser. She grabs Peter who is now fully recovered from his head injury. "You can direct me. I've no clue where this place is."

"No bother, Ma'am."

"You're taking your life in your hands. Have you seen the boss's driving?" says Jason.

"You wee baby. I've seen two year olds with more guts than you," says Shona.

They arrive at the church in one piece and Peter doesn't seem undeterred by the drive. The church would be picturesque if it weren't for the addition of a dead body, and what seemed like several hundred bobbies. There are also several vicars milling round, as well as a number of other people who shouldn't be there. Shona pushes her way through and immediately grabs her nose. The body has obviously been lying in the sun for several hours. Whilst the embalming has slowed decomposition it hasn't halted it completely. A stray animal, probably a fox, has been gnawing on one arm. Several hundred flies are also taking advantage of a free meal. It is not a pretty sight. The victim is a young man aged about twenty. Like the others, he is clean-shaven, spotlessly clean, with well trimmed nails and carefully combed hair. A cross adorns his chest and he is wearing priests clothes. What a way to end your life thinks Shona.

"Who found the body?" Shona asks the POLSA.

"She's over there." The local POLSA indicates a young woman dressed in a suit and dog collar standing next to a tree. The woman looks like she's just lost her dinner. Her colour is dreadful. In fact Shona has seen healthier looking corpses.

She approaches the vicar. The smell of vomit tells Shona she was right. "DI Shona Mckenzie. Can I ask you a few questions?"

The woman's glazed eyes turn towards Shona. She focuses. Swallows. "Yes."

"Could you tell me what happened?"

"I came here to get ready for the Churches Together meeting." She stops, then, her voice shaky, continues. "I found the body lying on the front step."

Although vicars are used to seeing the dead, Shona is sure, that the bodies are not usually in quite such a state. Or dumped on the steps of her church. The ecumenical meeting explains the number of vicars at the scene.

"Did you touch anything?"

"No I ran over here. I was sick and then I phoned the police."

Shona is thankful she'd had the nounce to be sick away from the body.

"Do you know the victim?"

"No."

"Are you sure? You've never seen him in the course of your duty?"

"No definitely not."

"Thank you. Could you give your statement to DC Roberts." She waves Jason over.

The crime scene, as with the others, has little in the way of clues. Concrete, baked hard ground and browning grass is not the perfect backdrop for leaving evidence behind. The team do what they can and then leave. Shona hasn't got far when she is accosted by the press. This time it's not Adanna. It's a pair of vultures from the local rag. Despite Adanna's willingness to conform, Shona still doesn't trust the press. Her opinion of them is that they are a swarm of undesirables out to make a quick buck on the back of other's misery.

"Shove off you pair. I'm not in the mood."

"But—"

Shona moves forward, puts her face up to the reporter's and says in a low voice, "Put one foot near this crime scene and you'll be singing soprano. Don't even think of arguing with me."

"You just threatened me."

"Sergeant Johnston, did you hear me threaten this man."

"I never heard you say a thing, Ma'am. He must need his lugs cleaned out."

Shona and Peter stride off with all the authority their positions give them. Before she goes she tells the PC's that they have permission to shoot the reporters if they twitch a muscle. The PC's are used to her, so just say. "Of course, Ma'am." Never mind the fact the Scottish police are not armed.

"Being a bobbie's a great job," says Peter.

Shona smiles. "I love it. No other career provides the opportunity to torment reporters."

Returning to the Gulags, Peter starts a search on HOLMES for their dead priest. Again no hits, so Shona sends for Double Eckie.

"You're keeping me on my toes Shona. I'll be wanting extra time for all this work."

"Name your price Eckie. You're worth it."

Once she has the photo, she sends it out to every division in Scotland. She's willing to stake her granny on the fact that the dead priest is dressed up and homeless. She's almost completed her task when she hears a voice.

"Shona, we're back."

She looks up to see Rory and Alice smiling at her. Alice comes rushing round the desk and hugs her. "We had soooo much fun. We went to the beach, and dug castles, and went on the merry go round and everything. Daddy bought us ice-creams every day."

"It does sound like fun. I missed you guys."

"You should have come with us Shona. Daddy says you work too hard."

"Does he now."

"Rory, you talk too much." Their father has joined them.

"Douglas, it's nice to see you." Her dazzling smile holds a hint of I'd like to do more than smile.

Douglas grins back. "Are you free to come for fish and chips tonight?"

"How could I turn you down? Give me a couple of hours and I'll be round."

When Shona goes into the office to dismiss the team Nina says, "By the look of your face I'd say the Procurator Fiscal and his offspring are back?"

"They most certainly are. You're free to go home to your nearest and dearest." Shona grows warm at the thought that some of her nearest and dearest have returned to the fold.

24

The surgeon prepares his tools. The trolley has been cleaned and is prepared for the next stage of the operation. Simple tools; two scalpels, one for the job plus a spare, stainless steel, polished and honed to perfection. Two packs of swabs are opened, twenty in each pack, and a spare pack placed on the trolley. A cauterising machine is added and plugged in. A cable leading to the operating switch at his feet is connected. That is it. A simple, yet crucial, task is about to be performed. The journey is almost completed.

Calm, dispassionate, professional, he views the body. A scalpel is picked up. The first decisive cut made. A purposeful stroke and fluid flows out, staunched by the swabs. A slight movement of the foot, and the machine whirrs into life. A gentle touch with the tip of the probe and the wound is cauterised. This is repeated until the perfect cross remains. The body is now ready for the next part of the journey.

25

Having had a pleasant evening with the Lawsons, Shona sleeps the sleep of the dead. Not that it's the best way to describe it under the circumstances she thinks. She decides to run to work to blow away the cobwebs. Her pace and the heat have her in serious need of a shower by the time she arrives. She has a dress in her locker; that and a quick shower and she looks presentable and ready to face the world.

"Turned intae a supermodel have we, Ma'am?"

"All glammed up and ready to face the day," says Roy.

"I'm glad you said that, Roy. I'm looking for a volunteer and you've just volunteered."

"What for? I never said anything."

"You're too cheeky by half. This little task should make you think in future. There's a group of twenty three schoolchildren coming to see what we do. You can show them round."

"You're not serious are you, Ma'am?"

"As serious as Ebola."

"I don't know anything about kids."

"Funny that, because your the nearest thing we've got to a kid around here."

"But, Ma'am—"

"See what I mean. You even sound like a whiney brat. Suck it up."

Resigned to his fate, Roy asks, "When and where?"

"Ten o'clock in reception. You've got them for

three hours."

"What am I going to do with them for that long?"

"Play Monopoly with them. What on earth do you think you're going to do with them? Tell them all about the wild things we get up to. The censored version. Then there's lunch laid on for them."

Roy cheers up considerably at the thought of grub. Little does he know it's a cheese sandwich and a fizzy drink.

Whilst Roy is entertaining a group of screeching ten year olds, an officer from the Police Investigations and Review Commissioner's office is interviewing Shona. Particularly galling is the fact that it is the Procurator Fiscal who has to make the decision to involve PIRC. Yes, her very own Douglas has set the hounds on her.

"DI McKenzie, thank you for joining us. I know you're busy but it is important that we get answers as to why there were explosives left in a public park."

As if I had any choice but to join them. I can't believe I'm sitting here listening to this pompous windbag, she thinks. As if I would leave them deliberately. Despite her belligerence her stomach is tight and she feels physically sick. This could be the end of her career. Not that it matters in light of the fact that a few teenagers have died.

"Can you please tell us about the conclusion of the case following which the explosives remained behind?"

Shona gives them a brief snapshot of what happened at Camperdown on the day they caught their suspect.

"Once you had the suspect in place what was done to ensure that the park was safe for the public to use?"

"The entire park was searched using both officers and dogs. However, given that the incident with the bomb was nowhere near the park it was not considered to be top priority. All evidence suggested that our suspect was using one specific area to sleep and nothing else."

"That will be all Inspector. We will be in touch if we need any more information."

Shona leaves with the knot in her stomach growing tighter.

Her day improves slightly when she gets back to the office. She receives news of their newest victim. He has been identified as Derek Davies, last seen in a homeless shelter in Glasgow. He hadn't been there for a few months.

"Two questions here. Why is someone killing homeless people? Why are they dumping bodies in churches in Dundee?"

"I've not got a scooby," says Jason.

"What are you talking about man? Can you youngsters no' speak English?"

"Scooby Doo, Clue," says Jason. "You've a cheek speaking about English."

"Remember I've a few years seniority on you son. Speak to me like that again and I'll find some nasty job for you to do."

"I've enough to worry about with you and Roy having a go at each other, Jason. Don't drag Peter into it too."

"It doesn't answer your questions either," says Nina.

"Someone's obviously got it in for the homeless, so we need to work out why. That would be easier if we could find a connection."

"Have any of the homeless shelters got anything or anyone in common?" asks Abigail.

"That's a good point. We need to interview the three shelters we know of. I'll do it through Skype.

Peter you can join me."

It takes longer than she thinks to set up the interviews. After about an hour she has arrangements in place to do them thirty minutes apart. The local police are setting the computers up in their interview rooms.

In the interim, they drive to St Xystus. As luck would have it, the drop-in is on that day. There is a buffet table groaning with food. Shona has to drag Peter away as he is eyeing up a huge slice of Dundee cake.

"No chance, sunshine. Keep your mind focused on the case. Anyway we've work to do."

She is given a paper cup of tolerable coffee. Peter is looking at his tea in disgust.

"This is so weak it needs resuscitating." Shona has to agree it doesn't seem to resemble tea as much as milky water. Dave Dickinson, who runs the shelter, is a twinkling-eyed gnome of about eighty.

"Welcome, welcome. How can I help you? Ask me anything you want. Always happy to help the police. I was in the merchant navy myself so know all about discipline."

When Shona can get a word in edgeways she says, "Have any of these men been in here?" She hands over the pictures.

He scrutinises them for what seems like centuries. "No. The vicar showed me the pictures before. There was one of a woman as well. Penny Smith-Lanson. Tattoos from hell, and I mean hell. Strange lass but spoke affy posh. None of the men though. I remember everyone..." He pauses for breath and Shona takes advantage of the gap.

"Could I have the names of the people who volunteer here? In fact include anyone who has helped here in the last six months."

"None of them would have done it. They all come

to this church. They're all good Christian men and women. Not a bad bone in their body."

Given the cross that's not much of a testimony, thinks Shona.

"I'm sure you're right but I still need the names. We can strike them off our list of suspects."

He rushes off to oblige.

"I think he's the only bloke I know who talks more than Roy," says Peter.

"I never thought he'd stop. Nice chap though."

"Oh, Chap." Peter mimics her English accent. "Penny's no' the only posh English woman round here."

The British Civil War is averted by the return of Dave and the list.

The first Skype interview starts at 1400 hours. Shona is speaking to a woman called Juliet, who runs the shelter in Inverness. Shona shows her the photos. She says that she remembers Kieran, but none of the others have been in. She doesn't recognise Penny either. She agrees to email a list of volunteers and paid staff. The conversation is repeated with Glasgow. The only thing different is the accent. Again, a list of volunteers will be emailed through.

Scrutinising the lists brings no eureka moments. Not a repeated name in a grand total of eighty two people.

"That's a lot of names," says Roy. "How many folk do they need to run a homeless shelter or a drop-in?"

"Quite a few obviously. No surprises that the main bulk of them are from the shelter. They would need to cover 24 hour shifts."

"Still doesn't help us though. Much as it pains me, we need to look at the church angle."

"We're no' going to interview those poor nuns again are we?" asks Peter.

"Not at the moment but I think we'll be driven to it eventually."

As Shona walks back to her office the Chief summons her.

"Shona, what's this I hear about you threatening the press?"

"I did no such thing, Sir."

"I've had a phone call saying otherwise. All I get is complaints about you."

"Don't tell me Pa Broon, or Vlad the Impaler times two, owns the Glenesk Recorder?"

The Chief's lips twitch. "What have I told you about nicknames. Give Ex Lord Provost George Brown the respect he deserves."

"I rather thought I was, Sir."

"Not only did you threaten to emasculate the reporters, you also threatened to shoot them."

"I certainly did not. I merely gave the PC's permission to shoot them. Given they don't have any guns it's not much of a threat. Surely the nation's press should know that we are not armed. I was just having a bit of fun with them."

"Get your fun off duty in future. That is all."

The Chief is definitely smiling as Shona leaves the room.

Shona comes up with a strategy for talking to the churches. They will start with the ones which have had a body dumped on their premises, and ask for a list of staff. Every last one of them is going to be checked out so thoroughly that the police will know the colour of their underwear. She calls the team together to let them know they're working late. She is half way through outlining her plan when she notices Roy is not following her speech.

"Roy is there somewhere you'd rather be? Are we keeping you from anything important?"

"Sorry, Ma'am. I'm thinking."

"Thinking? You looked like a zombie. Put the effort of your thinking cells into the case. Resign if you'd rather be somewhere else."

The team breaks up and starts to ring round the churches. Although it's later in the day, most of them have emergency numbers. Shona considers this enough of an emergency to ring them. They are all cooperative and give them a list of the staff who work there. This includes cleaners and maintenance staff, as well as clergy.

A couple of them come up more than once. One of them is Mo, their cleaner. She seems to be moonlighting at a couple of churches.

"I can't believe Mo's doing this. She's one of the nicest people I know," says Shona.

"She's been working here for about twenty years," says Peter. "I would vouch for her quicker than I would my kids."

"She'll have a key to the churches though," says Abigail. "It could be a member of her family."

"I can't beleive we're going to be investigating Mo," says Nina. "She's like a second mother."

"Sometimes I hate my job," says Shona. "Who else comes up more than once?"

"Reverend Barnabas James-Hunter. He seems to work part time at a couple of the churches."

"What's he doing in Dundee with a name like that?" asks Peter.

"We can't hold his name against him," says Shona. "The last I heard it wasn't illegal to have a posh English name. What churches does he work at?"

"St Xystus and Kings."

"Interesting. We need to have a chat with the

Reverend in that case. Roy, let your fingers do the walking and find out all you can about Barnabas. Abigail, you and I are going round his house."

"Do you not think it's a bit late to be calling on a vicar," says Peter.

"This particular vicar could be a mass murderer. I'm not too worried about his being in bed."

The vicar must be making a nice living from his two parishes. He lives in a grand house in East Haven. It has a view to die for looking over the expanse of the North Sea. It is lit in spectacular fashion by a low-slung full moon.

"If you're going to investigate murders then this is the best part of the world to do it in," says Shona.

"It doesn't come any bonnier than this," Nina replies. "It makes you proud to be Scottish. No offence meant, Shona."

"None taken. I consider myself Scottish."

They ring the doorbell. 'How great thou art' chimes through the house.

Nina starts giggling.

"I'm warning you, Nina. This isn't the time to be laughing."

Nina giggles more loudly then bites her lip at a look from the boss. Shona can see what looks like blood on Nina's lip but she doesn't care. As long as Nina looks professional when the door is opened. They ring the doorbell again. Cue for more lip biting.

The door opens as far as a chain, and a tall man, in a paisley dressing gown says, "Yes. Do you know what time it is?"

"DI Shona McKenzie and my colleague DS Nina Chakrabarti." She shows her badge.

"I can't see it. It's too dark."

"Then switch a light on."

"Is it one of my parishioners?"

"For Pete's sake look at our badges and let us in. It's too late for this. If you don't we'll arrest you and you can spend a night in the cells. Then we'll talk at a more reasonable time in the morning."

"How dare you! I am a Minister of the Church. You can't talk to me like this."

"Open this door or we'll break it down. That will give the neighbors something to talk about."

Barnabas quits arguing and opens the door. "I'm not happy about this."

"Duly noted. Is there somewhere we can sit?"

He escorts them to a lounge furnished in such a way that it wouldn't be out of place in a stately home.

They all sit down. Shona says, "Reverend James-Hunter, you may want to put some clothes on. Certain of your assets are swinging in the wind."

The Reverend pulls his dignity and his dressing gown together and leaves.

"There's a very suspicious smell in here," says Nina.

"I know. We need to have a look around."

When the Reverend returns Shona says, "I believe you work at both St Xystus and Kings."

"Yes. Why do the police want to know about that?"

He's either as thick as Scottish dumpling or he's bluffing, thinks Shona. The whole church has probably been in turmoil over the dead bodies decorating the front steps. In fact she's sure every church in Dundee is talking about it.

Nina, leaps from the chair and says in an urgent voice. "Can I use your toilet?"

"I'd rather you didn't. You won't be here long."

She sits down again and says, "As long as you don't mind me menstruating on your chair."

"Turn left down the hall. It's on your right."

Nice one, Nina. Shona is impressed. Nina has managed to hit on the one thing guaranteed to make this pompous peacock worry.

"You must have heard about the bodies which were found on the steps of St Xystus Church and Kings Church?"

"Yes. What of it?"

"Well you seem to be the only person who has something in common with both."

"That doesn't mean I murdered them."

"We are not saying you did. However, I do need to know where you were on these nights." She rattles of the dates.

"I will need to get my diary."

As he stands Nina returns. "That's better. May I ask you some questions Reverend?"

"I'm just going to get my diary."

"You can answer my sergeant's questions first."

"Why is your house stuffed full of Cannabis plants?"

Barnabas leaps up and makes a run for the door. Shona sticks out one long leg and trips him up. "Oh. I'm frightfully sorry." Nina has his hands behind his back and is cuffing him. "Where is that diary? You might want to bring it with you," says Shona.

It's one o'clock in the morning by the time they are finished and their reverend is in a cell. He's asked for a lawyer but Shona convinces him it would be better if he waits 'til the morning. Mention of an exorbitant call out charge for the middle of the night has him reconsidering his options.

"What a brilliant strategy Nina. I couldn't have done it any better myself."

"Because I took my mobile phone with me I was able to take photos as well."

"You're a genius. Now head home as we'll be back here interviewing him by sunrise."

"What. That's at about 0600 hours at this time of year."

"You know what I mean. Sod it. Let's have a bit of a lay in. Get here at 0930. We'll leave him stewing until we're ready."

"I'm leaving my phone with my mother. Anyone who tries to drag me out to a 4 a.m. crime scene will know an Indian mama's wrath."

"With that scary thought I'm sending you home."

26

The thought of Nina's mother's wrath must have kept their killer at bay. They both arrive bright eyed and ready to take on the world. Well, Barnabas James-Hunter anyway. Shona has left a disgruntled Shakespeare, whose frantic cries seemed to indicate that she was applying for adoption. She is quite unimpressed with the hours that Shona is keeping at work.

The pair grab a plate of bacon and eggs whilst Peter is busy elsewhere and then head to the interview room. The Reverend and his lawyer are in situ awaiting their arrival. Thankfully, it is neither Angus Runcie nor Margaret McCluskie. In fact it is someone whom Shona has never clapped eyes on before. It turns out he only deals with clients who are ordained.

The preliminaries over, Shona opens her mouth to ask a question. Before she can utter a syllable the lawyer leaps in.

"How dare you arrest my client. He is a respected member of this community, and has dedicated his life to helping others. What will this do to his reputation in the ministry?"

"His reputation? Are you having me on? Every room in his house is stuffed full of cannabis plants. A team went there this morning and he's even got them growing in the bathroom."

"It's for medicinal purposes. I suffer from a lot of pain."

"Tommyrot. With that amount of cannabis you're obviously dealing."

"Are you calling my client a drug dealer?"

"Yes, I am and I intend to prove it. However, that's the least of your client's worries. What we really want to discuss is the dead bodies which have appeared on the steps of both churches where he is an assistant Pastor."

"Are you saying my client is a murderer?"

"I'm saying no such thing. I'm saying we need to ask him some questions. Now would you be quiet and let your client speak. I haven't got time to be chewing the fat with you all day."

The lawyer takes the hint. Shona slides the diary over to Barnabas.

"Where were you on the following dates?" She repeats the dates she gave him the night before.

He looks and then, " I was at the youth club on two of the dates. I run them in both churches."

"In the middle of the night? Still it's convenient that you were already at the churches just before the bodies were dumped."

"What are -"

"Where were you on the other dates?"

"Nowhere. I was home."

"With only a bunch of cannabis plants as an alibi. That's not much good to you is it?"

"Why would I be murdering people?"

"Maybe they were customers of yours and were going to spill the beans?"

"You can't prove that," says the lawyer. "Where is this going?"

"It's going to a full investigation into your client's activities. In the meantime Reverend you're staying here until you appear before the Sherriff for playing a leading role in a Category 2 offence relating to the production of cannabis. I'll be recommending you don't get bail. If you're lucky, you'll go in front of the Sherriff today. Most likely it will be tomorrow." She pauses, leans closer to the suspect, and says, "That means you're with us for at least eight days. Plenty of time for me to dig into every single tiny aspect of your life."

She stands up. "Nina, take him back to his cell."

As he leaves, the Reverend says, "I will spend the time praying for your eternal soul."

"Whilst I appreciate that, you might be better praying for your own if you go to prison."

"Roy, did you turn up anything on Barnabas last night?"

"It would seem he jumps about from parish to parish, a lot. Not much else."

"Probably doing it to hide his indoor gardening habit," says Shona. "Write down the Parishes he's been in. I'll ring the local police. If their street supply of skunk has gone down since he moved, they might just have found their dealer."

"Brilliant disguise though," says Jason. "Who'd have thought a vicar would be dealing weed?"

"Think of all the young people he'd have access to," adds Nina.

"I don't want to think about that. We'll need to speak to the youth groups at both churches."

"As if we're no' busy enough, now we've got tae worry about a cannabis farm," says Peter.

"Peter, ring round the stations where he previously worked. Get your mates to do a bit of digging. See if they were suspicious of any of his activities."

"Jason, find out when the youth groups are on. I want you and Roy to visit them and have a chat. I'll square it with the youth workers or whoever runs these things." She pauses. "The rest of us are off to the canteen." She watches them, then laughs. "Your faces. The rest of us are off to ring the senior Pastors of

James-Hunter's previous parishes."

Shona is speaking to a friendly Pastor from St Aidan's Church in Kirkontilloch.

"Good morning Shona. How can I help you?"

"Have you ever employed a Reverend Barnabas James-Hunter?"

"We did, but he was only with us six months." The Pastor's tone is more guarded.

"We currently have him in custody. While he was with you did you have any problems?"

There is a few moments silence, then, "There was nothing we could quite put our finger on. He did his job but we were always suspicious of him. He seemed a bit too good to be true, and a bit too down there with the young people. It didn't seem natural though."

"He wasn't with you long. Did you ask him to leave?"

"No, he went of his own accord. It doesn't surprise me that you have him in custody though. There was always something not quite right with him."

"You say that he was a bit too friendly with the youngsters. Any chance that could be in a sexual way.?"

"No, nothing like that."

"What about drug use? Did that seem more apparent during his tenure?"

The phone goes silent.

"Hello. Are you still there?"

"Yes, I'm just running my mind back over that time. Now that you mention it there was a flurry of substance abuse. It died down so we thought it was just a phase."

"Do you think it could have been linked to the period that James-Hunter worked for you?"

"I'd have to look at my records to give you a

definitive answer, but I'd hazard a guess as to you being right."

"Thanks. You've been helpful."

Abigail and Nina had the same reaction from another three parishes in which he had worked.

"Looks like he's a right ba.....ad boy," says Nina with a grin.

"Well caught Nina," says Shona.

It's not often lady luck is on their side but she is today. Either that or God is on our side, thinks Shona. Both youth groups are on that night. The boys will be off on a jaunt to relive their youth.

"Why do I get all the jobs that involve kids?" asks Roy. "I've done my stint."

"Now, I think of it, it would be better if Abigail went."

Roy mutters, "Yes."

"Not because of your moaning, but it would be better if a woman went as well."

"I don't mind going," says Abigail. "I used to help at a youth club in Skye. Nothing to do with the church mind you."

"I doubt it'll be any different to any other youth club. A bunch of teenagers, high on testosterone and female hormones."

That evening Shona is being fed authentic African Cuisine by her Grandmother, when her phone rings. Please, not another dead body she thinks.

"Ma'am, it's Abigail. We're in Ninewells hospital."

"You're meant to be at a youth group. What's happened this time?"

"We've brought a couple of the kids up as they're injured. Jason's hurt his leg."

"Can't I send my team anywhere without turmoil

ensuing? I hope you haven't done anything to injure the youngsters?"

"It involved a human pyramid. The kids are okay. Just bruised."

"You were meant to be interviewing the kids, not killing them. I thought things would be fairly calm with you involved, Abigail."

"Sorry, Ma'am. We were doing a good job of putting the kids at ease. We've got some answers."

"Did you manage to get to the other youth group?"

"No."

"Okay, I'll sort it."

Shona arranges for Nina to pick her up. Her Grandmother doesn't let her go without a fight.

"Shona McKenzie, you are not going anywhere without food inside you."

"Gran, I'll be fine."

Arguing is futile. Her gran, as always, wins.

27

It is time to prepare the body. In many ways this is the most difficult part of the journey. Limbs no longer flexible refuse to cooperate. The master is gentle, patient, coaxes them in. Like a reluctant child the limbs initially refuse to cooperate. A slight tension and then capitulation. The body is dressed in a beautiful Bishop's robe. The master squints, uses his hand to protect his eyes from the reflection of the sunlight from the gold embroidery. A Mitre, the hat of a bishop, is placed on the dead man's head. It is adjusted until it sits at just the right angle. The material of the robe is straightened and smoothed. His master, God, deserves perfection.

The master picks up a pair of small, perfectly sharpened scissors. A slight nick is made in the fabric of the robe. A larger cut is made, then another and another. In precisely two minutes twenty seven seconds a hole is cut from the material over the chest. The cross is displayed for all to see. The master views his handiwork. The work he has done for God is good. He is part of his master's perfect plan as the savior of humanity.

Candles, in silver holders, are placed around the room. Each one precisely seven inches apart. They are lit, now that darkness is falling. The master dresses in opulent robes and becomes the high priest of the order. Prayers, never previously heard, are sung over the body. It is now fully cleansed and ready for the final part of its journey.

"Only the Lord can cleanse and save the lost. Call on him ye sinners, harlots and those who are defiled. No longer are you a part of this unclean world. You have been sent to the only place that you deserve because you refused to turn from your evil ways. Eternity will claim you."

This filthy wretch of a man has now been saved

28

The next day Jason is limping but returns to full duty. He's twisted his ankle but has been told to exercise it.

"I'll get you exercising it. You're going to be running around all day doing my dirty work for me. Only you could go to talk to a few kids and end up damaging yourself and them."

"I managed to look after twenty kids and keep them in once piece, Soldier Boy. The Army probably threw you out."

"No bickering. Roy, brief us on what you've come across on our boy Barney, and then you're off for the day."

"Off? Doing what?" He is rightly suspicious.

"Equality and Diversity training."

"What? Why?"

"Following your punch up with Jason about the quality of the sergeants and DI's in Police Scotland."

"That was months ago. I'm a changed man."

"That's as may be, but your still doing the training. Spit it out. I've a case to run and your course starts in 15 minutes."

Resigned to his fate, Roy says, "James-Hunter did his training online. He definitely has a theology degree, but its legality could be debatable. He works about six months for a parish and then moves on. There's nothing out there about why."

"I'd say that it's so no one finds out about his little sideline. Off you toddle now, Roy."

Once Roy has dragged himself away she continues.

"Now, the little matter of the youth groups. What's the deal there?"

Jason says, "We were taking part in a human pyramid competition and our pyramid collapsed."

"I meant the questioning not the injuries, Jason. I haven't got time to keep up with your social life."

"Sorry, Ma'am. The kids were divided on him. Some of them say he is the bomb. Other's say they can't stand him. That gang thought there was something creepy about him."

"I'll get uniform to take a wee look at the personal possessions of the ones who think he's the bomb. I've a strong suspicion it may contain weed. We had a similar response at the other church."

"There seems to be a lot of shenanigans in Dundee churches," says Abigail.

"That's no' true," says Peter. "Most o' the churches do really good work and support the community. Look at all the services they run to feed the homeless."

"Peter's right. The religious communities are a great bunch. There's the odd exception but I'm sure that's true, even in the police."

"Roy's the odd exception in the police," quips Jason.

"Very witty. You'll be joining him on that course soon. The question we should be asking ourselves though is, as well as being a successful cannabis grower, is he also a killer?"

"He seems a bit batty but we don't have anything on him to suggest he's our killer," says Nina.

"Your right. I want you and Abigail to go back through his history and find out every little thing about him. If he even did so much as pull the wings off a fly in primary school then I'm arresting him for murder."

"It's a great life working with you, Ma'am. You just arrest people and then think about it later," says Peter.

"Never mind throwing the book. You shred and bury it."

"I'll have you know everything I do is above the law."

"I know. That's what makes it so brilliant," says Peter.

Shona has not long started on the act of delving into Barnabas's past, when she is interrupted by Brian Gevers.

"I've not got much for you at the moment, Brian. My investigation is a bit stuck."

"We're all a bit concerned about Jock," says Brain. "No one's seen him in weeks."

"Peter says he sometimes goes walk about."

"I know, Ma'am. But we've had an alert out on him and no one has seen him in the Police Scotland area."

"Thanks for letting me know, Brian." Shona hotfoots it to the team office.

"I'm extremely concerned. Given that our killer is targeting the homeless, it's likely he's got Jock."

"Ma'am. If he's got his hands on Jock we need to catch him,' says Nina.

"Don't you think I know that? I'm as fond of Jock as anyone. The thought of him ending up like our victims is making me physically sick. This case has just stepped up a notch, from top priority to stratosphere. Peter, you're coming with me to interview James-Hunter again. I'm sure he's got something to do with this."

Barnabas is not in a talkative mood. His lawyer has advised him to keep his mouth shut.

"I'm sure you're right up to your dog-collared neck in this. It will be better for you if you help us."

The silence continues until Shona slams the desk.

"I haven't got time for this." It's not often Shona gets really angry, but when she does it's effective. "Someone I admire is missing and if I don't find him then I'm adding that to the list of charges I'm going to be hanging on you. If it weren't for the fact that it is now illegal, I'd be hanging you for them as well."

"I haven't murdered anyone. You can't prove it."

"Take that smirk of your face or you'll not be able to smirk again."

"You can't threaten my client."

"I wasn't, but I'll threaten you in a minute if you don't shut up."

There is a knock at the door and Nina enters. She hands Shona a sheet of paper, and leaves. Shona reads it and then says, "You're not such a fine upstanding man of the cloth as you would have us believe. It says here you were arrested ten years ago for assault to severe injury. You were plain Barry James then."

Barnabas's face turns white. He tries for bluster. "That's not me. That's not my name."

"For heaven's sake Reverend do you think we're stupid?"

"There's no need to blaspheme."

Shona's voice could crack glass it is so cold. "Listen here, Barnabas, or Barry, or whoever you are. Don't even think about lying or wasting my time."

"Okay. I was Barry James. But I turned my life around. I didn't want the old me to get in the way."

"It would seem the old you hasn't disappeared, just been camouflaged. Like a chameleon you adapt to any territory. Now, with the matter of the murders, have you anything to tell us."

"I'm not saying another word." That's the only thing he has said that morning that isn't a lie.

"In the meantime we're keeping you in our cells and we'll be all over your house like a dog on heat."

"Sir. The case is heating up." She explains her concerns to the Chief.

"If you are responsible for auld Jock's death, then not only will you be sacked, you'll be run out of town."

"I know, Sir." The Chief cannot make her more miserable than she already feels.

"Get this case solved, and do it now. It has taken far too long already."

"I'm going to see if the nationals and locals for Scotland will run something on Jock Someone, might know his whereabouts."

She is talking to the Chief's bent head. She leaves the office wondering if she could offer the Chief up as a replacement for Jock.

Such is the tramp's popularity that the *Evening Telegraph* runs it that evening.

'Dundee Stalwart Missing: Has the Crucifix Killer got Auld Jock?'

Despite the dramatic headline the article is fairly balanced. A little sensationalised but not over the top. It finishes with a plea for anyone who knows his whereabouts to contact Shona. It has Adanna Okafor's name against it.

"It's no a crucifix, it's a cross," says Peter.

"Cross Killer probably doesn't have the right ring to it," says Shona. "I don't care what they call it as long as we get results."

They have a few phone calls about Jock. One caller says they had seen him heading up towards Aberdeen. Another says he thought he was going through to Edinburgh, and yet another, the Sidlaws. Shona thanks them for their time and says they will look into it. She then phones the police in Angus, Aberdeen and Edinburgh and gives them the heads up. Then she heads home, her head spinning and her heart heavy. A large glass of Talisker takes away some of the sadness. Shakespeare, intuitively knowing something is up, cuddles close in comfort. Shona feels better if only for a brief moment.

29

The body, having been prepared and blessed is ready for transportation. It is placed on a bier, a movable trolley that carries the dead. From there it is transferred into a coffin, and this, in turn is transferred into a hearse. The coffin is moved so it sits squarely on the platform. Every move is suitably solemn. The master, now transformed into the driver of a hearse, takes the wheel. His assistant slides into the passenger seat. They bow their heads, and only then is the key turned. The vehicle coughs into life, and assumes a quiet purr. The hearse moves forward. The body starts on its final journey.

30

Shona is driving as fast as the law will allow without taking away her license. Her destination, St Bartholomew's Catholic Church in Linlathen. Her chest is tight and she is struggling to breathe. Please God don't let it be Jock. Please God don't let it be Jock, goes around and around in her head. She sees a blue light behind her and stops. She shows her badge.

"I've another dead body. It could be Jock."

"We'll blue light you there, Ma'am. Just follow behind."

She does as they ask and within minutes she is at the crime scene. Being the closest she is the first one there, apart from uniform and the POLSA. Sergeant Muir takes one look at her and says, "It's not auld Jock."

Shona sags against the pristine, white painted wall of the modern church. "Thank you." Then for good effect, "Thank you."

Then she feels guilty about being so relieved. "How can I be glad that someone has died. My only concern was for Jock."

"It's okay, Ma'am. I felt exactly the same way"

She pulls herself together and walks up to the corpse. A bishop, arrayed in his full regalia is perfectly arranged on the step. His outfit is complete with mitre and crosier, the ornamental crook used by bishops.

"I've heard of escalating, Sergeant Muir, but not by promoting the victims."

"We'll be looking for the Pope soon."

"Don't joke. The frightening thing is that it could happen."

Apart from the dress the victim looks much the same as many of the other corpses. This time Shona puts his age at about seventy. He is clean-shaven, hair neat and well combed, and everything else about him is immaculate. He has a small tattoo of a sun on one hand, and a moon on the other. They look to be recent, no older than about six months.

Iain joins her and Shona says, "Get as many photo's as you can. There are some tyre tracks in the dust. See what you make of them."

St Bartholomew's is a brand new building with beautifully maintained gardens. The priest is standing under the shade of an old oak. The church has obviously replaced a previous one.

"Father Jerome?"

"Yes."

"May I ask you a few questions?"

"Of course." The priest is calm and exudes a feeling of comfort and peace.

I bet his congregation love him, thinks Shona. He's the sort of man that you would always feel you could go to in a crisis.

"Do you know the dead man?"

"No. I found him when I came to open up the church for early morning mass."

"Does your church run any sort of drop-in, or soup kitchen for the homeless?"

"Yes, we do. It's open three mornings a week. It will be on today."

"I'm afraid you will have to cancel today. This is a crime scene."

"Of course. You may have some backlash from our service users this morning."

"We will deal with that."

"Did you see anyone else around when you arrived?"

"No. There was a black car turning the corner at the top of the road. I thought it was a hearse, but I might be imagining things. My eyesight isn't as good as it used to be. Age brings a lot of problems, my eyesight being one of them."

There seems to be a lot of pointers towards this being the work of an undertaker, in this case, thinks Shona. Or a vicar. Or both.

Shona is contemplating this, when her very own Procurator Fiscal appears.

"Shona, you really must stop killing people so you can see me. A simple phone call would suffice."

Her heart flutters and she whirls round. "Douglas. I wasn't expecting you to come."

"I've got my niece staying with me at the moment. She's thinking of studying at Dundee University so down for a visit from Inverness. My own resident babysitter."

Before Shona has time to reply, Whitney, the police surgeon dashes in leaving a slipstream in her wake.

"A bishop. You're certainly going up in the world." She bends over the corpse, does a few measurements and says, "Dead and embalmed. I can't wait to see what you come up with next. Bye Shona." She leaves them trembling behind.

"Was that a tornado I just felt?" asks Douglas.

"A tornado fighter jet I think. She's got some energy. She makes me feel old."

Back at the office they are all eating cream cakes. Even Peter has convinced her he needs one. Given that their brains are working overtime this is about the only thing which will drive them.

“More tattoos. Roy, did you manage to do a search on them?”

“Yep. Nearest I could come up with is they could be a symbol of pagan worship. There are also some strange articles which say that there are signs of Catholicism worshipping the sun and moon.”

“I think our dead chap is more likely to be worshipping Sunblest bread and Silentnight beds than anything else. Let's leave the Catholics out of this.”

“Shall I send out his picture to the homeless shelters?” asks Jason.

“Yes. We need to get identification. I'm a bit concerned that no one has come up trumps with a couple of our bodies though. How awful that no one is mourning their deaths.”

“How did the course go, Roy?” asks Shona.

“Mind numbingly boring but made me think. Think I'll behave so I never need to do the course again.”

“You needn't worry about doing the course again. Any repeat of that behaviour and you'll be kicked out of the force.” Shona's smile softens the words, but her tone indicates she is serious.

“Got it loud and clear, Ma'am.”

Shona's mobile rings, and she answers as she leaves. “DI Mckenzie.”

“It's the Duty sergeant.”

“If you tell me there's a dead body I'm likely to scream.”

“No, Ma'am. There's a laddie here says he wants to speak to you.”

She and Nina are sitting in an interview room with the laddie. He's about seventeen years of age and his name's Ryan. His mother has dragged him here and ordered him to tell the police everything.

“Ryan, you've got some information for us?” asks

Shona.

"I'm not sure."

"Tell us what it is and we'll decide."

"What if I'm wrong?" The laddie's knee is jerking fifteen to the dozen.

"We won't be cross, but we need all the information we can get. It might help us with the case."

"I go to the youth club at St Xystus." He stops and holds on to his knee.

"Yes." Shona encourages him trying to remain patient.

"Barnabas chats to me a lot, because I'm not as energetic as the others. I've got asthma."

Anticipation tightens Shona's stomach. This lad should write a novel the way he plays out the tension, she thinks.

"He offered me drugs a couple of times. Weed." He pauses, then, "I said no."

Shona's heart sinks. They've got him on the drugs but still no connection to the murders.

"He asked me if I'd like to meet a new group of Christians. One's who are the real deal. Doesn't like our Pastor much."

Shona isn't sure if this information is pertinent but she wants to make the most of having a willing witness.

"Do you know anything more about them?"

"I told him I wasn't interested, so he didn't say any more. He told me if I mentioned it I'd end up with a cross on my chest."

No wonder the poor boy is in such a state. He must have been carrying some weight around, thinks Shona.

"You've been really helpful Ryan. I need you to think carefully. Did he say anything at all about this other group?"

"Nothing. I'm not sure they're in Dundee though. He said once it took him a while to get to them."

"Thank you Ryan. Now don't you worry about this. Nothing is going to happen to you. I promise."

The lad looks a bit brighter and leaves with the hint of a smile on his face.

"We're no' any further forward," says Peter. He's been interrupted performing the important duty of reading *The Courier*.

"We've got something to speak to Barney about though. I know with every fibre of my being, that he's involved with these murders."

I wish you'd stop calling him Barney, Shona," says Nina. "All I can think about is purple dinosaurs."

"If you're going to tell me off at least say Ma'am. You might as well get it right. Now find the purple dinosaur and bring him to an interview room."

It takes a bit longer than they think because Barney insists he has his lawyer present.

"We have new information Reverend. A witness has come forward who says you tried to recruit him to a strange group."

"What a load of rubbish. These kids are always making things up. Who is this witness anyway?"

"As if I'd tell you that. The thing is, I believe him, and I don't believe a word that comes out of your mouth."

"It was probably Ryan. The lad has a crush on me. He propositioned me. When I knocked him back he said he was going to get me."

"How dare you turn this back on a teenager. You were in a position of trust."

"Which is why I turned the pimple-faced little snot down."

Shona bangs the table. "The only snot here is you. You threatened him."

"Prove it."

"Think about your future before you answer this question. Who is this mythical group?"

"How would I know? Ask him. It's all in his head."

"I know you're involved in this and I will prove it. See how you like twenty years in prison."

Shona feels like rearranging Barney's nice new dental work. She contents herself with moving into the Reverend's personal space, and saying, "I am going to be crawling through your life like maggots through a corpse. You wont be able to fart without me knowing, you despicable little git."

Barney is back in his cell and Shona has calmed down enough to hold a meeting.

"What do we know about religious groups in Dundee?"

"More than we did when we started," says Nina. "I feel like I'm swimming in them."

"Best to ask Uniform, Ma'am. They're the ones who know about comings and goings in Dundee."

"Nice one Peter."

"We've had a hit on our latest victim. His name's Tommy Anderson and he goes to a drop-in in Kirkaldy. He wasn't homeless but a bit down on his luck."

"I wonder if the Reverend has ever worked there?" asks Jason.

"Good question and you can find out the answer. I'm off to talk to Andy down in Uniform."

Andy not only has time to chat to her but also dispenses coffee. Well it looks like coffee but Shona wouldn't like to stake her life on it. She thinks it might actually be engine oil. She keeps quiet for the sake of interdepartmental harmony.

"Another trip to the weird and wonderful for you

then Shona? Dundee's very own grim reaper, Shona McKenzie, strikes again."

"Life would be boring without me, Andy. I need to pick your brains about religious groups, probably Christian, in Dundee and it's environs."

"I can tell you there are a heck of a lot of them. Anything more specific you'd like to know?"

"We've had a tip off that Barnabas James-Hunter might have been recruiting for a strange group. We're wondering if it might be related to our murders."

"Given the decoration of your victims, I'd think you might be right. There's nothing I can think of though. All our churches are well established and respected. There are a couple which are a bit bizarre but they don't tend to bother anyone."

"Bizarre is too mild for my case. Have you heard of anything outside the Dundee area?"

"No, but I'm fairly quiet at the moment. I'll ring round my mates and see what we can drag up."

"Thanks, Andy. I owe you a pint."

"I wont let you forget it. It's the annual barbecue soon. You can buy me one then."

"If I'm not working this case then I will."

Shona is busy reading about cults when Adanna Okafor appears at the door of her office. She is about to step inside.

"Take one more step and I'll arrest you. What are you doing here?"

Adanna stops but a beaming smile appears on her face. "I wanted to talk to you."

"How did you get up here?" The smile isn't fooling Shona. The press are only after one thing in her opinion, information. Which they will twist to make her and her team look bad.

"Andy is my cousin. I came to see him and he said

he was working on something for you."

"I jolly well hope he didn't give you any information about my case?" Shona is half way out of her chair.

"Chilax, Shona. He told me nothing. He's a good cop."

"Tell me to chilax again and you'll be revisiting your breakfast I'll hit you so hard. My day wasn't good but you're ruining it completely."

"I'm sorry. Look, I really do want to work alongside you. I know the press have been more of a sword in your side than a thorn but we're not all like that. I'm one of the good guys."

"I very much doubt that there are any good guys in the press."

"Give me a chance to prove it."

Shona grows silent. The woman does seem persistent, and she hasn't given any cause for concern so far, she thinks. Maybe she should give her a chance. She could do with all the help she can get.

"Could you do a search of the local and national papers for any religious cults which have set up? This is confidential mind. One sniff of it in *The Courier* and you'll be reporting from intensive care."

"Blimey, you like to threaten people a lot."

"I don't call it a threat, I call it looking into the future."

"I never thought I'd see the day," says Peter. "Shona 'Press Hater' McKenzie, inviting *The Courier* to help on our case."

"I'm that desperate I'll try anything. Besides, the whole of Scotland must know this is some sort of religious killing by now. What harm can it do?"

"Working with you is never boring, Ma'am," says Abigail.

"You certainly can't say this case is boring, stalled maybe, but not boring."

"After our last run in with reporters, the old adage, keep you friends close and your enemies closer might be true," says Abigail.

"Thanks for those words of wisdom. Have you any more sage advice to impart?"

"Confucius said, "Our greatest glory is not in never falling, but in rising every time we fall. That's quite a good one."

"I was being facetious, but he was a very wise man Confucius. We seem to do a lot of falling."

31

Shona hasn't had enough to drink. That and the heat have her reaching for Paracetamol. As she's rifling through her rucksack she comes across the leaflets they'd been handed in town a few days ago. She glances at them before throwing them in the bin. One is for a The Church of Glory and Worship of the Everlasting God. Never heard of them she thinks. The name alone makes her think they're up to no good. Grabbing a coffee to wash down the Paracetamol and stave off the headache, she opens her browser and does a search. The Church meets in an old warehouse on the outskirts of Brechin. From the website it would appear they are into Old Testament prophecy and snake handling.

The team seems to be doing very little in the way of investigating. In fact there appears to be more social media and newspaper browsing going on.

"Who fancies a jaunt to Brechin?"

They all look keen but Abigail gets the gig. "I can listen to more of your pithy sayings en route. The rest of you look into The Church of Glory and Worship of the Everlasting God. See if they've been up to anything we can investigate them for."

"Nuns, churches, is their anyone in the religious community you would like to leave in peace," says Peter.

"I'm leaving no one in peace until this case is solved,"

"Confucius says …"

"Zip it, Abigail. Confucius didn't have dead bodies in his patch. He had time to write sayings to torture people for millennia."

The old factory is looking quite swanky, as the Scots say. It has had a lick of paint and the inside looks fresh and new. There is one large meeting room with a stage, which is currently empty. Several offices are occupied. The place looks opulent. There's obviously good money in snake handling and prophecy, thinks Shona.

The Pastor is Ezekial Equinas, a tall, silvered haired man with a voice which would melt diamonds. Shona would bet Shakespeare on the fact that the money comes from a congregation of elderly widows.

"Reverend Equinas—"

It's Mr Equinas, but please, call me Ezekial. What can I call such a beautiful woman as yourself?"

His voice is making Shona forget Douglas. She pulls her gaze away from his and says, "Detective Inspector Shona McKenzie, and my colleague Detective Sergeant Abigail Lau."

"Welcome ladies. How can my humble church help you?"

"Could you tell us a bit about your church?"

"Of course." He lays out all the salient points and by the time he finishes Shona is almost tempted to join. He's hypnotic. Get a grip, Shona, she thinks. Abigail's eyes are glazed over so she pinches her.

"Thank you. Would you mind if we have a look around?"

"I can show you around. I wouldn't want you to end up in any of the rooms with snakes in them."

The walk around the site is enlightening. Three rooms do indeed contain snakes. Not in cages, but roaming free. They take one look and step back.

When the tour is over Shona asks, "Do you own

any more buildings?"

"No. This is it. You have seen my humble kingdom. Or should I say God's humble kingdom." He pulls out cards and hands them over. "We have a service on Saturday night. I would be honoured if both you ladies graced us with your presence."

"We are busy at the moment but maybe one day," Shona finds herself saying. She pulls herself together and asks, "Can we see a list of your members?"

"Of course. Ask my secretary."

The secretary is happy to comply and they are soon on their way clutching a photocopy of the list and the business cards.

They get into the car in a daze.

"What do you think, Ma'am?"

"I think he is the most compelling, hypnotic man I have ever met."

"I know what you mean. Do you think they're involved?"

"Every bone in my body is screaming that Ezekial is innocent. Thankfully my detective's voice is screaming louder. We're coming back here with a warrant, and a zookeeper to catch the snakes. I want to see if there's anything in those rooms he's trying to hide."

On returning to the concrete monstrosity in which they work, they peruse the list of members. As Shona suggested, they are mainly elderly women and a few young men.

"The men are probably looking for a sugar mamma," says Shona. "There's nothing in the membership to suggest they're killing some of them off. I don't think our dead men would be allowed anywhere near a church like this."

"If the dead men were elderly and affluent it might be a different story. Ezekiel could be killing them so he could have his way with the women."

"I like the cut of your jib, but it's not helping us much. Let's find a zookeeper."

A couple of hours later they are back in Brechin and searching through the snake rooms. The occupants, who are not happy about being disturbed, are in the back of a van, after a struggle and a lot of hissing. Shona is just thankful there aren't any spiders. She wonders if snakes eat them.

Ezekiel's usual sunny nature has slipped and he doesn't look too happy either. In fact at times he looks downright evil. "Those snakes are holy emblems. You should not be interfering with them. You will incur the wrath of God."

"I'll have to take that chance. I'm sure God will understand that I'm trying to solve a murder."

"God understands only His own Law. He will bring down his wrath on this sinful nation. I am the voice of God with a warning to the sinful. Turn from your evil ways."

Shona looks at him. Fury blazes from his eyes. Then he changes and the mesmerizing look is back along with the sultry tone.

The rooms are empty apart from different types of wood for the snakes to slither over and wind around. The exception is a small cupboard in each of the rooms.

"That's antidote in case anyone is bitten."

"I thought you lot think God will protect you?"

"We do. However, Satan may have entered one of the snakes and will use its body to bring us down."

They take one of the vials for testing and take their leave.

"They're all doolalie tap," says Abigail.

"I agree, they're not quite right in the head. I still don't believe they are in the business of murder. It doesn't seem their style. They'd probably just kill them with snake poison and say it was an accident."

It isn't long before Iain has the results of the contents of the vial. It is indeed antivenin. Another dead end.

Shona is thinking of going home. It's been a long day and she wants to get ready for her date with Douglas. She has a warm feeling in the pit of her stomach at the thought. It's not often she gets time alone with him. This, coupled with the thought of a meal at Bombay Joe's, makes her think she has died and gone to heaven. Peter coming into the room disturbs her romantic dreams.

"Ma'am, do you remember the laddie who went missing from Dundee University a couple of years back?"

"Can't say I do."

"His parents kept ringing and we investigated in the middle of a big case."

"I do seem to recall. It wasn't a big deal if I remember." Then she has a light bulb moment. Actually it is more of a dim glow. "Didn't he go off and join some weird sect somewhere in Angus?"

"He did, the Sidlaw's if I remember right."

"You went and searched the place and said everything was fine. They seemed genuine if somewhat cookie."

"I did, but you never know."

"We can investigate in the morning." Shona isn't breaking her date for anyone. "Besides, if a corpse is scheduled for delivery tomorrow morning, they are long dead and embalmed by now."

Shona looks up the address and decides to have a quick look around the perimeter before going home. It's not that far out of her way. In fact, nothing is that far out of anyone's way in Dundee. It's a small city and it only takes about twenty minutes to get from A to B, wherever you are going. By car of course. If you go by bus it seems to traverse every little lane, and takes hours. She points the nose of her car towards the Sidlaw Hills.

The Church of Perpetual and Only Truth took up residence in an old farmhouse about four years ago. They keep themselves to themselves, and apart from the missing teenager, Shona hasn't had any dealings with them. Still, it's always worth having a gander as her Grandmother would say. She drives through glorious scenery in the early evening sun. It is low in the sky, and she's having difficulty seeing despite the sun visor. A drive round the perimeter shows nothing untoward, so she turns the car down a leafy country lane and heads home. She hasn't gone far when a huge four-wheel drive comes towards her, turns round and blocks the lane. Something doesn't feel right so she stops, slams her car into reverse and immediately crashes into another vehicle. There is a sound of crushing metal and her seatbelt stops her short. A muscle mountain runs towards her and pulls the door open. Shona reaches for the gun she doesn't have. He claps his hand over her mouth and the world goes dark.

32

The men move quickly and soon have Shona in the back of the vehicle which is still in one piece. One of them picks up a phone.

"I need a job done." He gives the location and the nature of the job. "It's highest priority. I want no trace left."

"We're on our way," comes the disembodied voice from the phone.

Shona's body is transported at speed, one man making sure she stays asleep. This is fortuitous, he thinks. An opportunity such as this does not fall into your lap every day. As they drive up to the gates of the community, they unlock. A highly sophisticated security system links both gates and car. The gates swing shut as they enter. They drive to the holding building. Shona is transferred inside. She is handcuffed and then locked on to a hefty metal chain. This leads to a secure bolt in the wall. The prisoner will not escape.

The men leave, locking the solid metal door behind them. They go to find out their master's plans.

33

Peter is at home with his feet up on a pouffe, drinking tea and looking at the hole in the toe of his socks. He's taking advantage of the fact his wife's out to devour a couple of chocolate hob nobs. Goodness knows how many of these he's allowed on the plan, but he's knackered and doesn't care. You're beginning to feel your age Peter, he thinks.

"Dad, I'm off to Lindsey's. I'm having a sleep over."

His daughter swoops in to kiss him and then flies out the door. At eighteen and in her last year at school she'll be following her brother to University later in the year.

Peter picks up the telly remote and switches on the football. He sees one kick and then the phone rings.

"I wish Sally's mates would stop ringing her day and night. It's like a telephone exchange in here. Why we got her that mobile phone I'll never know, she never uses it," he announces to the empty room.

"Hello. Sally's not in."

"Peter. It's Mac. I'm the duty sergeant tonight."

"It's half past nine at night. Don't tell me you've a body. I'm too exhausted to attend a crime scene."

"No. I've got a puzzle. The DI seems to be missing."

Peter sits bolt upright, his tiredness forgotten, and switches off the television.

"What do you mean missing? She set out about three hours ago to get dolled up for her date."

"The Procurator Fiscal's been on the phone four times. She never turned up. She's not answering her phone. He's been round her flat and she's nowhere to be seen. Her car's not there either according to him."

"Get anyone in a Police car to go out and look for her. I'll ring my lot and get them in."

They are all gathered in the office, each one trying to put on a brave face. It's not working.

"We need to contact her neighbour," says Nina. "She'd never go anywhere without making sure the cat's okay. She might leave Douglas high and dry but not the cat."

"Jason, get round there and ask the neighbour. If the neighbour has a key look round the flat. See if there's anything to indicate she's been hame and gone again," says Peter.

"I'll go with him," says Nina. "I'm not sure a man's gonna be able to work out anything in a woman's flat."

"Off you go then. Ring me the minute you have an answer."

The answer is no, Mrs Gordon hasn't seen Shona and yes she would look after Shakespeare. The answer is also that the flat looks like there hasn't been anyone there since the morning. Shona is definitely missing. Peter tells them to get back pronto. They need to start a hunt. He turns to the rest of the team.

"Right..."

Before he has a chance to continue Douglas Lawson crashes through the door.

"Have you heard anything? Is she here?"

"I'm afraid not, Sir. We're—"

"What are you doing to find her? Shona wouldn't go off. You know she wouldn't."

"Sir—"

"Douglas. It's Douglas. We haven't got time to be formal."

"Douglas, we haven't got time to chat either. I need to get a plan together."

"I'll help."

"You're in no fit state to help. You need to go home and look after your kids."

"The kids are fine. I'm staying."

"That's…"

"I'm staying."

"Okay, but I'm in charge. You need to let us do our job. With all due respect we've got more experience wi' these things."

"Agreed."

"Right, as I was saying. Can anyone think of anywhere she might be? Anything to do with the case maybe?"

"The snake church weren't very happy about us interfering with their snakes. In fact Ezekiel was downright nasty about it. I think he's a nutjob," says Abigail.

"Do you think he's enough of a bampot to kidnap Shona," asks Nina.

"I don't know. She is a woman and he seems to think he has a hold over women. Maybe he wants her in his harem," says Abigail.

"That church is rolling in it," says Roy. "I had a look into their accounts."

"How did you manage that?" Peter looks impressed.

"You don't want to know. Let's just say he's a multi-millionaire. I don't think the DI has enough money for them to be interested."

"He might think we are looking into where he gets his money. We asked for a list of members."

"That's a definite possibility then," says Peter. "Make it number one on the list."

"Why are you all sitting here talking about this? We need to do something," says Douglas.

"We are doing something. Running off half cocked isn't going to help us find her. We need to work out where to go. We'll end up exhausted and useless if we don't have a plan of action."

"Where else could she be?"

"Why don't you sit down and think about anything she's said to you in the last few days. It might give us a clue."

With Douglas occupied, they continue.

"Do you remember that lot up the Sidlaws? The ones that student went to join."

"Barely, but yes," says Nina who has joined them. "What about them?"

"I reminded Shona about them earlier. She said we'd go and talk to them in the morning."

"Highly unlikely to be them then. They won't even know we're investigating them."

"True but we'll add them anyway."

"The Alexyev twins are always threatening to off her," says Roy. "They might have seen a chance and taken it."

"It could be anyone." Douglas's voice is getting louder. "She's alienated half of Dundee."

"Has anyone told the Chief?" asks Iain.

Everyone looks blank. Peter picks up the phone. The Chief is soon on his way. He requests a driver as he has had a drink. Peter asks Douglas if he would oblige as he needs everyone on the team. Douglas agrees.

"I know the poor man is upset but he's not helping much," says Nina once Douglas has left.

"We need tae keep civil about the PF. We all indirectly work for him."

"I'm more worried about Shona than his feelings."

"Has anyone got any more ideas about where she could be?" asks Peter. "We need to get a move on."

"Claypotts, Ratray and Elgin could be involved," says Roy. "She's rattled their cage so much it's bound to be broken now."

"Mac's pulled most of his officer's back. They all like the DI," says Peter.

Brian Gevers comes hurtling through the door, followed by the Chief in a more stately manner. Douglas, a pathetic figure, trails behind.

"What is going on here? I leave for a minute and the Inspector manages to cause more chaos." The look in his eyes belies the roughness of his tone. He's as worried as the rest of them. "What's your plan?"

"While it's light, all personnel, CID and uniform will be out searching. We've narrowed it down to a few areas," says Peter.

"Get the search started now. I will stay here manning the phones. If she returns I will call," says the Chief.

"What can I do?" asks Brian.

"You can go in a search team with Sergeant Chakrabarti. Do exactly what she says."

By this time there are more uniform turning up. "Everyone get stab vests and guns," says Peter. "CID will be heading up the teams. Follow their orders."

There is general chaos for a few minutes until Nina takes charge. "Listen in. You, you, you and you, go with Roy."

Roy waves his hand and they all move off. She repeats this until the only person remaining is the Chief. He goes to his office and pulls out a bottle of brandy. He needs a drink to get through this. He picks up the phone to make an unwelcome phone call. The Chief Constable of Police Scotland is not happy to hear one of his best officers is missing. He tells Thomas, aka the Chief that he is on his way. Thomas screws the top back on the bottle of brandy and puts it back in the drawer. Better not to be drunk when the most senior police officer in Scotland arrives. Especially given the circumstances for his arrival.

34

When Shona awakens she finds herself in a prison. Handcuffed and shackled to the wall. Her exploration tells her that she is in a barn. It is dark now. How long has she been here? A few hours or a few days? Disorientated she can't work it out. She tries to think. Feels around. The earth is damp but she is not wet. She hasn't wet herself then. So that means it is hours. She does need to pee though. No, don't think about that she tells herself. She tries to recall how she got here. Her head hurts, and she feels like she is in a fog. Where was she earlier, and what was she doing? She has a vague memory of leaving work. She was meant to meet Douglas. What happened on the way that brought her here? Her breathing quickens. This is not good. She forces herself to breathe slowly, to take in what fresh air there is.

Then she feels the first tickle of an insect against her leg, then another, and another. No, not spiders. Anything but spiders, she thinks. She doesn't have many fears but this is one of them. She screams into silence. It is muffled by concrete walls. The insects are coming towards her face. She snaps her mouth shut. tries to brush the insects away. It is futile.

She is praying for death when she hears a trembling voice. At first low, then louder.

"Shona? Shona is that you?"

The voice takes her mind off the insects. "Jock. Oh

thank God. Jock are you okay?" Tears fill her eyes and she swallows. "I've been worried about you."

"I'm no really okay. They killed Maggie." His voice breaks and he starts to sob. Maggie is his little dog, a gentle Scottish Terrier who he'd named after his dead wife. Shona is devastated for him.

"I'm so sorry Jock."

"Why did they have to kill her? She never hurt anyone. She loved everybody. She would have stayed with me even in here. The only time I've heard her growl was when this lot grabbed me."

"Jock, in this darkness, how did you know it was me? Surely you don't recognise my scream?" Talking to Jock is helping take her mind off the insects.

"I recognised your perfume. You always wear bonnie perfume."

Well I never thought a bottle of Sarah Jessica Parker's Dawn would come in so useful. Thank you Sarah Jessica, thinks Shona.

"I'm glad you did Jock."

"I was waiting for you to come. I knew you'd come."

"I'm not really the saviour of the world here, Jock. I'm in the same boat as you. We need Superman or Spiderman to swoop in."

"I thought that might be the case." Jock sounds sad. "I dinnae like the thought of a bonnie lassie like you being in here."

"I can't say it's doing much for me either Jock. Still, at least we've got each other."

"You'll still get us out o' here Shona. I know you will."

"I'm fresh out of heroic inspiration Jock. I'm desperate for the loo. That's all I can concentrate on."

"I've a bucket in my stall. You probably hae one as well."

Shona fumbles around and finds the bucket. Thankfully her legs are free and she's able to stand up.

Ablutions finished, the place falls silent. Then Jock speaks.

"Shona. What's happened to the others?"

"What others?"

"There were a few others laddies in here and they've all gone. They took them away and they never came back."

"I'm not sure, Jock. We'll work it out later."

"I think there's another young lassie in here, but she's gone awfy quiet."

A soft voice, devoid of all hope, says, "I'm still here."

"Shona's a detective, she'll be able to help us."

"What use is a private detective? Anyway, I heard her say she's a prisoner as well."

"I'm a police detective. They'll be looking for me. What's your name?"

"You're still a prisoner. It doesn't matter what my name is. I'm going to die anyway."

"She's called Elspeth."

"Elspeth. I am going to get you out of here. None of us is going to die on my watch. Now, we need to get some sleep so we've strength to fight another day."

Having reassured everyone else she still has to deal with the spiders. Now that it is quiet she can almost hear them scuttling around. She moves, can feel the spiders on her. Bites back a scream. She doesn't want to traumatise Elspeth. The spiders skitter over her bare skin, dancing on her nerve ends, causing pain she never realised she could feel. She moves into the corner, her back on the bare cement wall.

"Are you all right lass?" Jock, even in the midst of his own torment, is still thinking of her.

"I'm fine Jock. Just trying to get comfortable." The

tremble in her voice gives away the truth.

"Keep talking to me, Shona, We'll get through this together."

"Jock, you need to get some rest. You'll need all your energy for when we get out of here."

She pushes her back further against the wall. It offers little protection. She prays she will get through the night. This truly is her dark night of the soul.

35

Peter, and his gang of uniforms are searching the area around the Church of Glory and Worship of the Everlasting God. Having had to travel to Forfar the light is beginning to fade. The warehouse is locked up tight as is every other building in the industrial estate. Shona's car is nowhere to be seen. There is a movement and they shout. A scruffy young lad runs away. They chase him until he disappears through a hole in the fence.

"Go after him," says Peter, indicating a young PC. The copper disappears through the hole in hot pursuit. Phillip and the others split up and go in opposite directions. He is caught coming through the fence on the other side.

"Right son, what's got you running for your life?"

"I was scared." The lad is going for belligerence.

"It's pretty obvious we're police. The word Police in great big letters on our vests is a bit of a giveaway."

"You could have been playing at it."

Peter takes his gun out of the holster. "I've got an investigation going on. I've not got time to champ my gums with you. Why did you run?"

He's holding a rucksack close. One of the PC's grabs it and empties the contents on the ground. Several cans of spray paint fall out.

"Looks like we've caught a graffiti artist," says Peter. "Take him to the local nick."

One of the PC's peels off and obliges. He grabs the lad by the back of the neck.

"Oi, that's assault."

"Shut it. You're in deep sh…"

"PC Grange. Don't swear at the lad." Peter has no illusions the minute they are around the corner that the lad will get it with both barrels. It will do the little vandal good.

All the teams systematically search the whole of Dundee. Shona, or her car, is nowhere to be seen. Roy's team does a sweep of the area around the foot of the Sidlaw's but it's getting dark.

"I can't see a beggaring thing," says one of the PC's. She could be dead in a ditch and we'd miss her."

"Less of the dead," says Roy. "The DI can look after herself. Wherever she is, she'll be fine. I pity whoever took her if that's what's happened." He doesn't know whether he's trying to convince them or himself. Despite the fact the boss seems to have a down on him, he likes and respects her. The thought of anything happening to her is unimaginable.

They all return to the station. The Chief is still there but hasn't heard from anyone.

"The Chief Constable is on his way from Inverness." The Chief is not looking good.

"Sir, I think you should go home. You look exhausted," says Nina.

"I'm staying until Sir Malcolm Rennie gets here." He will not be moved regardless of what is said. Nina wonders if she should have an ambulance on standby.

The PC's are all sent home and only CID remains. Peter tells them all to go home, he'll stay with the Chief. Nina, isn't for budging either. The rest are told to go and be back at 0700 ready for a search at first light. They refuse, and say they will doss down in the cells. Peter can't convince them otherwise. He tells Mac and says to heave them out if he needs the cells.

"I think we might give the Dundee criminal fraternity a free pass tonight."

"I think that's the right move."

Sir Malcolm Rennie doesn't arrive until gone 3 a.m. "There was a smash on the A9. Traffic was at a standstill. Has Shona been found?"

"Not yet, Sir Malcolm. We searched as much of the area as we could before the light fell. We'll be starting again at first light."

"That's excellent. I can see you have it all under control."

"Would you like a coffee?" The Chief stands up and then clutches his chest. He sits back down. His breathing is labored.

Nina picks up the phone to call an ambulance. They are there in record time and the Chief is carted off to Ninewells.

"I guess that leaves me in charge until the Chief Superintendent arrives in the morning. I'd rather like that coffee now."

36

Shona has managed to get a few fitful hours sleep. Dawn is breaking, bringing with it the first scorching heat of the day. When she jerks awake a rat is running out of the opening to her stall. She manages to stop from screaming, not wanting to disturb the other occupants. There are thankfully no spiders to be seen apart from one very dead one about a foot away. She shudders and turns away. She slowly sits up. Her chest hurts like a bitch. Probably from the seatbelt gripping her during the crash. She takes in her surroundings. She is in some sort of gigantic storage shed. The ceiling reaches far above her and the end walls are some distance away. It seems to be divided into a number of stalls. She can see the one opposite through the large opening at the end. There is a large ring high up on the wall. Chains hang from it. They end near a yellow bucket. This room is obviously ready for another occupant. The dividers between the stalls are wooden. The floor is earth, now mainly dry. She could have sworn it was damp last night. Incarceration must be getting to her. There are windows high up in the walls. No escape there.

She turns her attention to the chains, which are keeping her captive. Thick, solid links form a sturdy rope of metal. These chains mean business. Inexplicably they are highly polished. Buffed to a glimmering shine. Who on earth would polish chains intended for imprisonment? Where the chuff am I, she thinks. The handcuffs are standard police issue. In fact they really are police issue. Someone in the police is involved in this. She hopes it isn't anyone from her team. She rethinks that and decides it's definitely not anyone from her team. She would trust any one of them with her life. In actual fact, at this precise moment she is trusting them with her life. The thought of ending up the same way as her victims makes her physically sick. She rushes to the corner and vomits. The first time in her career.

"Shona, are you okay?"

"I'm fine Jock. Just a little bit too much to drink last night." The lie comes easily. She doesn't want him to worry about her. Also, she must have been drugged or chloroformed or something as she genuinely can't remember how she got here.

"I could do with a drink though. I take it they do give us fluid."

"Aye, They'll come in soon enough. To tell you the truth you'll have more fluid than you ever wanted."

"What?"

Before Jock can answer the rusty metal of the lock can be heard and the door opens. Elspeth starts whimpering. Before Shona can draw breath to comfort the girl, a jet of water is aimed through the opening of the stall. Shona jumps up and tries to avoid it. It is relentless and powerful following her wherever she goes. She coughs, splutters and tries to draw a breath. Just as she thinks she is going to die the jet stops. She can hear sounds from next door. Auld Jock isn't as agile as her and he screeches in pain.

"Leave him alone. If you have to do anything then come back to me."

"The figure ignores her. He finishes with Jock and moves on to Elspeth. The girl wails and then starts coughing. She sounds dreadful. Shona thinks the young woman is going to choke. The water stops and the hose is dragged away. It sounds like it is being coiled and stowed. Then there is silence as the figure leaves.

"What was that all about," asks Shona.

"You'll find out soon enough. I wouldnae know how to explain." Jock is sounding much more confidant than he did last night. Having Shona there is obviously giving him hope. I wish I had hope, thinks Shona.

The man returns. This time he is wearing brilliantly coloured embroidered robes. Shona wonders how he is able to carry the ginormous open book he has clasped in his hands. He starts to read whilst walking up and down the aisle between the stalls. His voice is loud, confident and clear. This is a man who is comfortable and sure of his role.

"You are but a filthy wretch, says the Lord. Turn from your evil ways. Turn from your sin, and I will save you. Those who do not turn to me will perish. They will perish in the flood…"

The voice continues for what seems, to Shona, like hours. It finishes with, "They will be branded with my cross and sent to the gates of hell. There they will be damned to burn forever."

The man leaves again.

Shona is stunned into silence. What on earth was that?

"Shona, are you there."

"I am, Jock. I'm just a bit stunned. What was that and where are we?"

"He reads that bit from his bible three times a day."

"That doesn't sound like anything I've ever heard in the Bible."

"I'm a Christian, lassie, and I can tell you he's made up his own Bible. I get the feeling he's trying to cleanse us."

Shona's voice is urgent. "We've got to get out of here, Jock."

"You don't need to tell me that. What's your plan?"

"I haven't quite got one at the moment, but the minute I do, you and Elspeth will be the first ones to know."

"I know you'll get us out of here Shona. You would never let me down.

Blimey Jock, I've enough on my plate without you treating me like some sort of hero, she thinks.

37

The team is up at dawn and swigging copious amounts of black coffee to jolt their systems awake. Doreen and Annie from the canteen have got wind of what's going on. They appear, like angels, carrying trays of sausage and egg rolls. They all, including Peter, gobble them down.

"It disnae taste the same without Shona giving me grief," says Peter.

"I'll be glad when her caustic wit returns to the head of the team," says Abigail.

"If she returns." Jason is gloomy.

Roy leaps from his chair and grabs the front of Jason's shirt. "Don't say that. The DI will be back. You're jinxing it."

Peter and Nina intervene. Peter somehow remains calm and says, "You're like a pair of two year olds. Do you think she'd want you fighting? I know feelings are running high but we need to work together."

They both return to getting themselves outside a couple of rolls.

The Chief Superintendent appears and says that Sir Malcolm Rennie is on his way back to Inverness. He has an urgent meeting there later in the day.

"He went via the hospital. Thomas is fine. They think it was angina brought on by stress and exhaustion. He's had a good nights sleep and wants to come back. They are keeping him in for another day to make sure he gets some rest."

"Those poor nurses," mutters Nina. Abigail digs

her in the ribs.

Twenty minutes later, when the sun has finished rising they are ready to go. They've used some of the hygiene packs supplied to the usual occupants of the cells, but they still look like they've been on duty for a week. Given the heat they don't smell much better but no one cares.

Peter says he and Roy will stay to interview Barnabas again. The Alexyev's are also on their interview list.

"I'd rather be out looking for the DI."

"I know you would but this is just as important. I can't interview the Alexyev's without some muscle."

"Borrow some muscle from Uniform."

"There needs to be two of us there. Now stop the incessant arguing. Mac's boys are escorting the Alexyev's here while we stand champing oor gums. The more time we waste the less likely we are to find the boss."

This galvanizes Roy into action.

Barnabas is not happy at having been woken so early. "It's 5 o'clock in the morning. This is police brutality."

"Did your mummy no' teach you to tell the time. It's 6 o'clock."

Barnabas opens his mouth.

"I'm no' interested in what you have to say unless it's an answer to my question. Now, our Inspector's missing. Do you know anything about this?" asks Peter.

"Even a thicko like you must realise I've been stuck in here for days. How, the hell could it be anything to do with me?"

"Watch your mouth. If you know anything it would be better to tell us now. If I find out you've hidden something that could have led to her being found you'll no' need to worry about prison. You'll be at the bottom o' the Tay Estuary."

"I can't say it any differently. I don't know where she is!"

"Stop shouting."

"Well you seem to be deaf."

Roy can't take any more of this. He leans over the table and grabs Barnabas by the shirt collar. "Listen here you supercilious bastard. If you don't spill the beans I'll kill you before the Sergeant gets to you."

"This is recorded. You will go to jail for this."

"Unfortunately there was a malfunction just before this happened. Now what do you know."

"Put him down, Roy." It isn't said with much conviction.

Roy complies. "We're wasting our time with this worthless bag of crap."

"I'm inclined to agree."

While he is getting up, Barney trips over the chair leg and goes flying. Thankfully the video was working again at that point to prove it was his own clumsiness that caused the problem.

The interview with the Alexyev's isn't any more helpful.

"I am glad she has gone," says Stephan. Or is it Gregor. They never can tell them apart. "But we did not do this. I would like to shake the hand of the man who removed her. I will pay him many rubles."

"Are you saying you paid to have her removed?" asks Peter.

"No. But I would like to congratulate the person who did this and reward him for his ingenuity and planning."

Roy whispers, "We've nothing against them, Peter"

Peter has to agree. "You are free to go."

Nina has managed to get hold of a warrant to search The Church of Glory and Worship of the Everlasting God. They had taken battering rams as they didn't think anyone would be there. She rings the bell out of politeness and Ezekiel answers.

"Don't listen to his voice, Nina," says Abigail.

Nina throws her a surprised look and continues. "We have a warrant to search these premises. Please let us in." She flashes both the warrant and her badge.

Ezekiel studies the document and then smiles. It's like the sun has dawned all over again. "Please come in ladies. My church is yours."

Nina looks mesmerized.

"I told you so. You shouldn't have listened to that voice."

They have brought the zookeeper from Camperdown with them again. He's moaning that he might as well move to Forfar. They ignore him and let him catch the snakes. Then twenty coppers go through the building. They find nothing.

"I hope you find your Inspector, ladies. Such a lovely young woman. I would like to welcome her to a service sometime."

"You'd better start praying we find her then."

Jason and Iain have gone to the funeral parlour of Claypotts, Ratray and Elgin. This time the battering ram is necessary. None of them have Shona's ability to pick a lock.

"I feel a bit strange battering down the door of a funeral parlour," says Jason.

"Me too," Iain agrees, "But we need to think of the DI. We need her back."

"She's the best boss I've had."

The door is open and within a few minutes the

burglar alarm is screaming like the hounds of hell. It won't be long until Ratray or Elgin appear. Claypotts is still tucked up in one of their cells. There are a lot of corpses in the place but no sign of Shona having been here. Elgin tips up and is not impressed. "What have you done to my door?"

Iain shows him the warrant.

"You could have phoned. I would have let you in with a key."

"Time was of the essence. In fact it still is. Come on Jason," and they leave an angry undertaker standing on the steps of his business, in front of a broken door.

"We'll send someone to fix it," Jason calls over his shoulder.

38

Shona doesn't have a plan. What she has is a splitting headache and a raging thirst.

"When are we likely to get a drink?"

"Sometime soon he'll come back with water, and something to eat. It's usually not much but it stops us from starving. I don't think he wants to kill us."

Little do you know, Jock. Keep that innocence. Shona's chest is tight with trying to keep the truth from the others and stay positive. What she wants to do is weep.

"What do you think they want to do?" asks Shona.

"Tame us. Make us join his cult. The ones who are the most worn down go."

Cult. Shona tries to remember why that is important. It tickles at the edges of her mind and then dances away again. Maybe when she has something to drink it will come back. Her brain is fogged. I'd give my right arm for a couple of Paracetamol she thinks. On second thoughts, perhaps best not to think like that. She could lose more than her arm at this rate.

She hasn't heard Elspeth since the soaking. "Elspeth. Elspeth. Are you okay?"

Silence. "Talk to me Elspeth. Come on. I'm going to get you out of here. I promise."

Shona listens and hears a faint whimper. Then an ethereal voice says, "I want my mum."

"Elspeth, were you homeless?"

Nothing.

"Elspeth, answer me. Get a grip girl. I need some

answers if I'm to help you."

The sharp tone works. The girls voice is slightly stronger. "Yes. Yes I was. I am."

"Why, were you homeless? Did your parents die?"

"No. My parents were too strict. I couldn't do anything. I ran away from home." She pauses and starts crying. "I want my mum."

The tears are a relief for Shona. At least she is showing some signs of emotion. The thought of seeing her mum again might keep her clinging on to life.

"The minute we're out of here you can ring her. I'll get one of my officers to bring you a phone. You just keep thinking about that."

"I knew you'd help us Shona. You're such a kind lassie," says Jock.

"Have you got any relatives you'd like to see, Jock?" asks Shona.

"I've a son from my first marriage. We split up when he was one and his mother wouldn't let me see him. Not that I blame her. I was a wild lad then. A typical squaddie. Foul mouthed, the temper of the de'il himself and drank all my wages."

Shona is astonished. She's had many a conversation with Jock and this is the first she's heard of this. "Maybe we could look for him when we're rescued."

"Aye, maybe. Do you think your team will find us?" Jock's voice is sad again.

"Of course they will. I've trained them well. There's no way they're leaving us here. They know I'd kill them if they didn't ride to the rescue.

"I'll be affy glad to see them."

"They'll be so glad to see you too. The whole of Dundee is worried about you. In fact we've had the whole of Scotland on high alert looking for you."

"Have you? Why would you do that?"

"Because we all love you, you old coot. Life isn't the same without you. I need you to drop-in and keep an eye on me."

Jock's voice quivers as he says, "I never knew that. I thought you were just being kind to an old man."

Before this love fest can go any further the door grates open. The man has now unrobed and is wearing neatly pressed trousers and a Polo shirt. It's like a fashion show. Every time he appears he's in something new thinks Shona.

"The Great High Priest of the church asked me to bring you your victuals."

What is he going on about, thinks Shona? It's the same bloke. Or is it? Maybe it's triplets. Maybe he's a good actor. He'd have to be a fricking good actor to keep this up for any length of time. Then it strikes her. He's got Dissociative Personality Disorder or Multiple Personality Disorder as it's more commonly known. It's the same man, but its not. The thought makes her bowels churn. If this is the case then their captor is on the edge. He could turn any minute, without warning, and one of his personalities is a cold-blooded killer. Not only that, he thinks he's on a mission from God. She prays that God will send her team in the right direction, and make it quick while he's at it.

39

Peter has to answer a call of nature and when he gets back Roy is sitting at his computer.

"What are you doing now? One minute you can't wait to get out of the door, and the next you're on Facetwit or whatever it is. Come on. We've work to do."

"I've had an idea," says Roy. "Can you give me twenty minutes max to look a few things up?"

"You've got till I make and drink a cup of tea. Do you want one?"

"Please." He is frantically tapping away at his keyboard.

Fifteen minutes later he emerges. Peter is frantically looking at his watch. "Get a move on Roy. We've got to get going."

"This was worth the wait. Our boy Barney hasn't worked in all the places where the victims are from but he's worshipped there."

"I'm still confused. He was in here when the last body was found."

"I don't think he was our killer, but I think he was feeding the victims to him or her."

Peter, thinks for a minute. "Do you know what, Roy. I think you've got it. So he knows who our killer is."

"I'm one hundred percent certain he does."

"Get him to an interview room now. If he doesn't answer my questions, for the first time in my career I'm going to beat the answer out of a suspect."

"I'll hold him down for you."

They have just got him into an interview room when Nina and the rest of the team reappear.

"Nothing to report I'm afraid."

"Our computer expert here, has cracked a bit of the case open." Peter indicates Roy. "Barney and the victims have all been to the same churches. I'd say that's more than a coincidence."

"Go Roy. You're useful for something then."

Roy grins and takes a bow.

"We're off to interview him again."

"While you're doing that, Jason and I will go do a sweep around the Sidlaws."

"You might want to see if there's any activity in the Church that moved into that old farmhouse up there."

"Will do." She and Jason leave.

Abigail sees Peter with a truncheon, and works out what they are about to do. "Peter, it's not worth it."

"Yes it is. If we find Shona I don't mind doing a stint in the nick. Not that I think the judge would send me there. He likes Shona."

"You've kids to think about. Plus Shona will not be happy when she finds out."

He puts the truncheon down. "Come on Roy." He puts one foot in front of the other like it takes great effort.

40

Shona feels numb. She takes the food, her mind whirling. She is given a couple of large bottles of water. Plastic so no weapon. She opens a bottle and guzzles it down. Some spills down her chin and on to the still muddy floor. Slow down, Shona she thinks. You need this water to recharge your brain. She drinks in a more measured way. The water is cold. It has obviously been refrigerated. Whoever this man is he wants to take care of them. Well at least one personality does. She doesn't want to think about the other ones. The water slides down her parched throat, soothing it. She takes another gulp and then stops. She contemplates the plate. A slice of what looks like home made, wholemeal bread, a hunk of cheese and a small apple. Not a lot but at least it's something. She wraps the bread around the cheese and lifts it. She pauses half way to her mouth.

"Jock, the food isn't drugged is it?"

"I don't think so. I've never had the jandies after it."

"What are you talking about? Why can't anyone speak English?"

"I've never been sick."

"What about sleepy? Have you ever fallen asleep after it?"

"No' that I'm aware of. I've barely slept since I got here."

"What about you Elspeth?"

"I've already finished mine and I'm fine."

Shona picks up the food and gobbles it down. She

didn't realise how hungry she was. It might be simple but it could have been a king's banquet.

She's no sooner finished than the Great High Priest is back. She prepares herself for another jet wash but this time it's just the walking and the praying.

"You are but a filthy wretch, says the Lord. Turn from your evil ways. Turn from your sin, and I will save you. Those who do not turn to me will perish. They will perish in the flood…"

It's the same passage but with an added prayer at the end. Change their eternal souls O God. Thou art all-powerful and can change these weak humans. Change them as you changed me. Bring them to you I beseech thee O God."

He finishes the prayer and leaves.

"Does he ever say anything else," asks Shona.

"It's pretty much the same thing all the time. I think he's playing a mind game. If we hear it enough then we'll change our minds and join his church."

"I'd say if I hear it enough I'm likely to go batty. How have you put up with that for weeks?"

"I don't listen to him any more," says Jock.

"Neither do I," Elspeth adds

Shona has to get out of here. She'd either be insane or dead if she stayed here much longer. Possibly both.

She has a plan.

41

The interview with James-Hunter is not going well. They might as well be interviewing the purple dinosaur for all the good it is doing them.

"So I was at the same churches as those men and women. They liked me and followed me up here for a better life."

"I think you were grooming them. Bringing them here like lambs to the slaughter."

"That is ridiculous. I keep telling you I am a respected man of the cloth."

"You were running a cannabis farm."

"Allegedly. Every time you mention this I say I was growing it for medicinal purposes. I have pain."

"In industrial level quantities? I find that hard to believe. I think you're a lying little weasel."

"Prove it."

Peter doesn't quite have the DI's aptitude with the cutting remark. He does, however, have a healthy dose of righteous anger. He leans in close and says in a low voice. "I intend to. Then I'm going to tell the general population of Shot's Maximum Security Prison that you're a kiddy fiddler. You're life will be worse than hell. I hear they cut the offending articles off."

"You can't threaten me. The video's running."

"Threatening you Reverend? I was merely listening to you. Your voice was so low I could hardly hear you. So you were saying you are ready to help us?"

Before the prisoner has a chance to reply there's a knock at the door. It is Nina. "Sergeant Johnston, I need to speak to you for a moment."

The urgency in her voice convinces Peter.

"DC MacGregor stay with our prisoner."

"What's up Nina?"

"We've found some headlight glass on one of the back roads leading up to the Sidlaws. It looks like there was an accident. Iain says there are flakes of red paint on the glass. They could be from Shona's car."

"Have you found her? Is she okay?"

"We don't know. Iain did a search for blood but there was nothing."

"Do you think she's been abducted?"

"I'd say so. The only inhabitants around are the weird church lot up at that farm."

"Get the team together. Call Mac, or whoever's on now. We need plenty of backup."

Peter enters the interview room. "Take this piece of scum back to his cell."

"What's up?" Roy takes one look at Peter's face and does as he's instructed.

Peter goes to find the Chief Superintendent.

"Sir, we think we have a lead on the Detective Inspector. It looks like she's been abducted. We need a warrant to search a church which has taken up residence in an old farm in the Sidlaw hills."

He provides a succinct overview of the situation so far. Just as he finishes the Chief walks in.

"Thomas, you are meant to be in hospital. What are you doing here?"

"They discharged me. They said I was fretting so much I was better off here. I would not stay in a hospital bed when my senior detective is in trouble."

Peter is dumbfounded. He'd thought the Chief hated Shona. You never can tell what's going through someone's mind, he thinks.

The Chief Super says, "We'll sort this out between us. I've a handle on what's going on and will bring you up to speed in roughly half an hour. I'm just about to drive to the Sherriff's office and get a warrant."

Peter is even more dumbfounded. He's never seen a brass do anything in the way of helping before.

"Would you like a drink, Sir? I'll get one of the PC's to bring you one."

"Earl Grey please."

Peter goes to find a PC who knows how to make it. He then tells everyone to move to the briefing room as there are about 35 officers milling around, all acting like they're on speed. It's going to be fun and games giving this lot firearms, he thinks.

42

The Chef is busy pulling bottles from four large fridges. Bottle, after bottle, after bottle, he places them on a scrupulously clean stainless steel counter top. It is the finest fresh orange juice. He pours it into row after row of plastic glasses. A carefully measured amount in each glass leaving a space at the top.

When this task is done he puts the bottles into plastic bin bags and carefully ties the tops. He drops them just outside the back door. Opening a smaller fridge he takes out several large bottles containing a clear liquid which looks like vodka. He uses a medicine pot to measure five mls, which is then placed in a glass. This is repeated until all the glasses are filled. Not one drop is spilled. The Chef makes sure that everything is as it should be and then leaves.

The Great High Priest enters the room. He opens the doors wide and rings a bell. As a line of disciples forms he welcomes each one.

"Now is the time for the final sacrifice. Today you will be with God. Our work here is complete. The father of light and the father of darkness will welcome you home. "

Each disciple takes a glass and leaves. Mothers take one for their children. The line is moving towards the place of sacrifice, a large field with an altar at one end. As the cocktail is drunk, the glass is thrown in a bin and the person sits down. Mothers help their children to drink the poison laced juice and then hold them close and soothe them. One by one their last breathe is taken. Not a sound is uttered, other than an occasional wail from a child. Soon all is silent. The sun is the only witness to this grizzly scene.

Once the last disciple is gone the Great High Priest places the four remaining glasses on a tray. He picks this up and walks towards his final destination, careful not to spill a drop

43

"Quiet," bellows Peter. What a racket he thinks. How Shona deals with this so calmly he doesn't know. She says it's like herding cats. He'd rather herd a cat any day than deal with a load of testosterone fuelled coppers going on a raid. He once again thanks his lucky stars that he never reached the dizzy heights of inspector. Shona must have the patience of a saint or a self destruct button, thinks Peter. It makes him even more determined to find her and bring her back to her rightful place. If that were possible. The racket dies down but there are still pockets of chatter.

"I said quiet. Anyone who is having problems with their lugs can go back to their desk."

That gets their attention and silence descends.

"We think we know where the DI is. It looks like she's being held up at the Church of Perpetual and Only Truth. They're the weird lot up in the Sidlaws."

"Why would a church be doing all this?"

"That, we don't know. Like I say they're weird. We won't know until we find the DI and arrest whoever abducted her."

He pauses for effect and then, "You're going to be armed. Some of you will have pistols and some rifles. It's a big area. Shoot only when necessary and to save your own or someone else's life."

"Can I have a rifle?" asks Jason.

"As you already know how to use one, then the answer is yes. Keep it safe and don't use it indiscriminately."

"Got it Sergeant."

"Go in small groups to get your weapons but make it quick."

Once they are back he hands them a list. "These are the teams you are in. There is one CID officer leading each team. When you get to the farm you will be placed strategically around the perimeter fence. There are five entrances and I want them all covered." Roy has done a stupendous job on Google Earth. They know exactly what the farm looks like, although it doesn't take account of underground bunkers, if there are any.

"Any questions?"

The silence tells him there are none.

"Right. It's time. On the bus, and we're no' coming back without the DI."

The Procurator Fiscal leaps on the bus at the last minute. "You're not going without me."

Peter thinks it's a waste of energy and breath, arguing.

44

Shona is going to get them out of here. At least she is going to get herself out of here. Then she will release the others. She has a party trick that always went down a storm in the police training academy. She can get out of any pair of handcuffs known to man, using a Kirby grip and her teeth. There's only one little problem with this plan, which is why she hasn't done it before. She can't get hold of a Kirby grip. There is one in the back of her hair. It is tucked up right at the back of her head holding a stray piece of hair up inside her plait. So it's hidden and fiddly as all get out to get to. She can barely do it with her hands free.

She twists her hands behind her head but can't quite reach. She tries again. And again. Each time adrenaline allows her to stretch a bit further. She is almost there. She stops to gather her breath and her strength.

"Are you okay Shona? You're grunting."

"I'm fine Jock. I've a plan to get us out of here but I need to concentrate."

"I'll leave you to it then."

She starts again, creeping ever higher with each attempt. She can reach the Kirby now but can't quite grab it. She resolves to grow her fingernails when she gets out of this place.

"Shona, are we really going to get out of here?" Elspeth's voice is trembling.

"We are sweetie. Just give me a bit of time to get it sorted. I promised you didn't I?"

"Yes."

"Well I never break a promise. You can introduce me to your mum when she gets here."

She's just about got it. One more go and she grips the end. The Kirby won't budge. Several more attempts and still no joy. She tears at her hair. It's painful to get it out but she doesn't care. Adrenaline dulls the pain. At last she has a grip and pulls. The Kirby falls to the ground. She grabs it, bends it, and sticks it in her mouth. She doesn't think about the dirt that is going in with it. She can worry about that later. It takes her seconds and four swift moves to get one of the handcuffs undone. Once she has a hand free the other quickly follows. She's out.

"I'm free." She is about to go and free the others when she hears someone coming. She runs out of her cubicle and grabs a plank of wood which is lying on the floor.

"Shona," says Jock.

"Hush. I need you both to be really quiet. I'll be back to get you I promise. You'll be out of here in no time. Please keep silent."

She positions herself behind the door. It creaks open. The Great High Priest steps in carrying a tray of glasses. She uses every ounce of power and strength she can muster and batters him in the face with the wood.

He screams, and falls to the ground. The glasses scatter, the liquid seeping into the ground. Shona leaps over him and is out of the door running like the hounds of hell are about to devour her. She can hear the High Priest, or whatever personality he now is, running after her. She is hoping that the robes and the blood running down his face will slow him down. She's also praying that one of his personalities isn't an Olympic athlete.

As she runs it all comes back to her. She's at that strange church up in the hills outside Dundee. She needs to get out of the compound and head down towards the city. Her legs move in fluid motion. She ignores the fact she is in sandals. She cannot think of that. She just keeps running. She has no clue where she is going but can see a fence in the distance. Where there's a fence there's a gate she thinks. The gate might not be sensible though. It could be manned. She hadn't actually thought how she was going to get out of the compound.

She can hear the man's feet thundering behind her, his breathing heavy and labored. She takes steady even breaths. In, out, in, out, taking in the maximum amount of oxygen, pushing out the right amount of carbon dioxide. She's a trained runner. This is natural to her. She reaches the fence and runs along it. She inspects it as she runs, looking for any break where she can get out.

45

The bus arrives at a country lane about half a mile from the camp. The teams file off. Each officer is silent, tense, and ready to move. The team leaders set off and their team members follow. They are slow and watchful. They don't want to startle anyone in the camp. They know there will be guards at every gate. They have seen the guard towers on the plans. Using trees as cover they creep forward. Silent. Not a word is uttered.

Peter takes Douglas. "Do exactly as I say," he says keeping his voice low and his tone even. "I know you're my boss, but if you want to see Shona again, I'm the one in charge."

"Got it."

They move towards the front gate watching for movement. Looking in every direction, their weapons at the ready. They see nothing. No movement. In fact, no sound either. An eerie silence covers the place like a shroud. They say it's like this in Auschwitz, thinks Peter. This gives him a feeling of pain in his chest. Please God don't let this be an extermination camp. Please let us find Shona alive.

As they approach the gate they stop. Binoculars are raised to Peter's eyes. Douglas snatches them.

"There's no one there," says Douglas.

"I can see that," Peter replies. "Why would the main gate be deserted?"

"Maybe they're in a church service," says one of the young bobbies.

"If they are, then it's the most quiet one I've ever come across. Even the Catholics are louder than this and we're not keen on a load of jumping around and singing."

They are still contemplating the gate when a figure bursts through the trees. They all cock their weapons and move.

"It's Shona," yells Douglas. He starts to run.

"Lower your weapons." Peter follows the Procurator Fiscal.

They see a man wearing a multi-coloured robe break through the trees. He is obviously after Shona.

"Police. Stop where you are," shouts Peter. He once again has his weapon ready, as do the coppers.

The man takes one look at them and heads in a different direction.

Shona reaches the gate. It opens easily. She runs through and throws herself into Douglas's arms. He clutches her so hard she has difficulty breathing.

"Not so tight, Douglas."

He releases his grasp slightly but still holds her tight.

The rest of Peter's team has set off in hot pursuit after the priest.

Shona pulls away from Douglas and starts to follow.

"Where are you going? Let them sort it out."

"No frickin way. After all I've been through, it's my collar." She starts to run.

Douglas bolts after her. There's no way he's leaving her now. He wants to protect her for the rest of his life.

Whatever demons are driving the priest are giving him supernatural powers in the way of running. Blood is running into his eyes from the head wound Shona had given him earlier. Even Shona's beginning to flag but the man just keeps on going. The others are now in the compound and have joined the chase.

"Don't shoot," shouts Shona. "He's unarmed and mentally ill. Watch your backs though. He's dangerous and thinks he's on a mission from God."

Eventually, they have him surrounded and that's when they find out he is also strong and violent. He lets out a bellow and tries to break through. When he finds he can't, he punches Jason in the stomach. Jason falls to his knees and vomits. One of the coppers meets a similar fate. Another is punched in the face.

Shona can see some of the officers getting their weapons ready. "Hold your fire," she shouts.

At the sound of her voice the priest turns towards her. This gives them a momentary advantage and they seize it. Several of the team wrestle him to the ground. Their suspect pulls a few more punches, but eventually he is cuffed and flat on the ground. A couple of burly policemen are sitting on top of him to keep him down.

"Get a van and a doctor up here. They need to sedate him or we'll never get him to the station." She glares at the officers. "Don't hurt him. He's not right in the head and I don't think he knows what he's doing. Keep an eye on him though. I don't want him breaking free again."

"Thank goodness that's over," says Peter.

"It's not over yet. Auld Jock and Elspeth are chained up in one of the buildings. Call a couple of ambulances." She sets off again.

"Who's Elspeth?" asks Peter to her retreating back, then follows her.

46

Jock and Elspeth are waiting for her.

"Shona, thank goodness your back. What's happening?"

"What's happening is you're safe. And free." She produces a key for the handcuffs.

"Free the lassie first. She's in a terrible state."

Elspeth is, indeed, in a terrible state both mentally and physically. She looks like she's been freed from a concentration camp. Every bone in her body is protruding and she is covered head to toe in filth. Exactly what this filth is Shona doesn't want to think about." Roy, give me your shirt." He silently takes it off and hands it over. Shona helps Elspeth put it on. Little does she know that she is starting her new life of freedom wearing one of Ralph Lauren's most recent designs. She can barely stand so Shona gently helps her up. The girl clings to Shona, sobbing. Shona holds her close and lets her cry. She beckons Roy over. "Give me your phone." He passes it over. She's never seen Roy so compliant.

She hands it to the young girl. "Phone your mum. When you're finished I would like to speak to her."

Elspeth dials, then listens. "Mum. It's Elspeth." her voice is weak. She starts crying and can't get another word out. Shona takes the phone.

"This is Detective Inspector Shona McKenzie."

Shona listens to the worried voice at the other end.

"No she's not in trouble. Far from it. Your daughter is an amazing young woman."

Elspeth's mother breaks in again.

"Why is she crying? That's a long story. She needs you here. I'm taking her up to the hospital. Take my number down. When you are getting close to Dundee station then ring me. One of my Officers will collect you and take you to the hospital. I'm going to be looking after her."

Another pause, then, "She is going to be all right. She needs you now. I'm going to send a car to your house. Hang on ..."

"Has anyone got a pen and paper?" She copies down the address and assures the woman the car is on its way to take her to the station.

An ambulance arrives and Elspeth is taken off to Ninewells.

Shona turns to Jock. He looks worse than he usually does, if this were possible.

"Jock you're a sight for sore eyes." She gives him a hug. She doesn't care about the fact he smells like a sewer and looks like one. He also clings on.

"They're going to take you to hospital. No arguing. Do what the medical staff say."

"For once I'll be glad to be indoors. Even if it is a hospital ward."

Shona has a word with the paramedics. "This man is a hero and he's been through a lot. Tell the nurses he needs a single room. If they don't comply tell them I'll arrest them for crimes against humanity."

The paramedics know Shona, but they know Jock even better. "If they don't they'll be needing one of our ambulances."

Shona musters up a weak smile. She takes Jock's hand and squeezes it hard.

"I'll see you up there, Jock."

"Thanks Shona." He gives her what passes for a smile.

Douglas says, "Are you going to come now?"

"No. I'm worried about the lack of people here. He can't have been running this place on his own. It's impossible."

"Shona you're in no fit state to be working."

"Well I am working. I'm not leaving here until I finish the job."

"I agree with him, Ma'am," says Peter. "You need to get checked out."

"I didn't realize that they took my rank away whilst I was incapacitated. When I last looked I was still an Inspector and the only person who can order me around is the Chief. Is he here?"

"No, Ma'am," Peter replies.

"Well I guess I'm still working. Is anyone coming with me to check this camp out?"

"In the absence of the Chief I am in charge of you Shona."

"Don't take this the wrong way Douglas but, wrack off. Now, are you coming with me?"

47

Moving slowly through the compound they look around them watching for snipers. Shona has grabbed a gun and a stab vest from one of the female officers who were dispatched in the ambulance with Jock and Elspeth, so is back in full Inspector mode. The first building they come to is clinical. The sun, bouncing of stark white walls, blinds them. Holding her hand to her eyes Shona takes in the scene. A steeel table with drains, a trolley and a strange contraption. A pristine linen cloth on which lie several knives and a scalpel covers the top of the metal trolley. Shona lets out a breath she didn't know she was holding.

"It doesn't take the brains of Einstein to figure out what happens here."

Peter crosses himself. "I dinnae even want tae think about it."

The others are transfixed.

"Move," says Shona. They pull their eyes from the room and comply. The stealthy search continues. They are skittish, ready to bolt at the falling of a leaf. Their eyes scan in every direction. Nothing moves in the still summer air.

They reach a large house, which could be the main building for the sect. Shona indicates everyone should stop.

"Get your weapons ready."

"Ma'am, do you think it could be wired for bombs," asks Jason.

Shona stops, her hand half way to the door.

"Everyone get back, as far away from the house as possible."

They start to move and then stop as they realize Shona is not following.

"What are you doing Shona?" asks Douglas. His face shows that he knows exactly what she is doing. "We all need to move, including you."

"Not a chance. I'm going in."

"Then I'm coming with you."

"No way. You've got kids."

Douglas hesitates and Shona opens the door. She's through before anyone knows it and is moving through the house. The others hurry to catch up. In the end they needn't have worried. There are no booby traps and no people either.

"He couldn't have done all of this on his own."

"Maybe they're hiding in the chapel. There has to be a chapel in a set up like this," says Nina.

They hurry through the vast grounds. The picturesque chapel is tucked behind a grove of apple trees. Its beauty belies the macabre reasons for their visit. The building is silent and empty. However, the bright sunshine, pouring through the windows highlights the scene in extraordinary detail. Behind the altar, displayed together, are a cross and a pentagram. The walls are painted in both Christian and Satanic symbols.

"What's that all about," asks Peter. "I've never seen Christian and Satan worshipers in the same house before."

"Our suspect has multiple personality disorder. He believes he's both God and Satan," says Shona.

Roy lets out a low whistle. That seems to sum it up.

It isn't long before they discover why the compound is

silent. The whole population of the complex appears to be sleeping together in a large field. Tall Scottish Pine trees line the periphery, hiding the scene from prying eyes. Birds twitter in the sunshine, a contrast to the otherwise eerie silence. Shona fears the worst. They check the pulse of first one and then another and another. All are dead. They stop when it becomes apparent that they are too late.

"Call ambulances," she shouts as she turns a young woman on to her back.

She is about to perform CPR when Roy shouts, "No. Stop. We don't know how they died."

Nina joins in, "If they've swallowed something contact could kill you."

Shona rocks back on her heels. "We've got to do something."

They all stop in their tracks as they hear what sounds like a thin cry.

"What was that?" asks Abigail.

"It sounded like a baby crying," Shona is already desperately searching amongst the bodies. The others join in.

"I've found it." She pulls an Asian baby girl of about six weeks old from under the body of what is probably her mother. "Get another ambulance." She cradles the baby close.

"You're not very clean Shona. You might want to hand her over," says Nina.

"I am not handing her over. Give me your shirt." Nina has a t-shirt on under her designer shirt. She gives it to Shona without complaint and Shona pulls it over her head. The minute it's on she takes the baby back.

"How come she's alive," asks Jason. "Every other person here has bit the dust."

"How the heck are we meant to know? Maybe her mother wanted her to live. It's no use speculating."

Shona has an eagle eye on the babies condition. She does appear healthy other than wailing.

"Has anyone got any bottled water?"

Roy pulls an unopened bottle from a rucksack. He hands it over. With a snap of the seal breaking, the bottle is open. She dribbles a few drops into the baby's mouth and she sucks strongly. Seems healthy. Probably starving, she thinks. The first ambulance arrives and Shona and the baby climb in the back of it. Douglas joins them.

The paramedic reaches for the baby.

"No way, Sunshine."

"We need to evaluate her condition."

"Evaluate away, but this little girl is staying in my arms."

"Shona, hand her over. Let the paramedics do their job," says Douglas.

With great reluctance, Shona complies. She crouches down beside the stretcher.

"We can't get near her with you there."

Shona ignores them.

"Peter. We need to deal with all those bodies. You're in charge, " she calls through the door. Get Whitney and every other doctor you can think of up here to certify the deaths. Who deals with mass casualties like this?"

"Nae need to worry, Shona. I'll sort it out. You just look after yourself and that wee bairn."

With that the ambulance doors close and a siren starts.

48

When they reach the hospital Shona hands the baby over and agrees to treatment herself. She asks Douglas to fetch her some clothes. He strokes her face, kisses her and complies.

As he's leaving she says, "Douglas." He stops and looks back. "Thank you for everything today. I'm glad you were there. Seeing you made things a whole lot more tolerable."

The sadness drops from his face and that dazzling smile appears. That alone makes Shona feel better.

She has some pictures taken for legal reasons and then is examined. After that they let her have a shower before the cuts on her feet and arms are dressed. They lend her a gown and a dressing gown while she waits for Douglas to reappear with fresh clothing.

She asks if she can visit Jock and Elspeth.

Elspeth is sitting up on the trolley with a drip in her arm. Her clothes are gone and she has a gown on. Someone has made an effort to give her a wash but it hasn't gone very far.

"How are you doing?" She holds the girl's hand.

"I don't know. The Doctors are doing a lot of tests. I don't know what any of them are or what they're for."

"I'm sure the nurse will explain if you ask. It might be better to just relax and trust them. They know what they're doing. The medical staff in here are excellent."

"When is my mum getting here?"

"I'm not sure, but I do know she's on her way. We'll be picking her up at the station and bringing her straight here."

"I wouldn't be here if it wasn't for you."

"That's not true. You're stronger than you think."

"I was ready to give up and die. You gave me courage. Made me feel I could carry on."

"That courage was in there in the first place. I just helped you to find it. Elspeth can I ask you a question?"

"What?"

"How did they get you up to the complex?"

"An old man said I'd be looked after there. He said they'd give me food and somewhere to sleep. I was living rough so I went. He was like a Priest or something, so I though it would be okay."

"Did you meet him at a youth club?"

"Yeh. How did you know that?"

"Just a hunch." I'm going to string Barney up by the toenails she thinks.

Elspeth's eyes are closing.

"You have a sleep. I'll be back to see you when you're in the ward."

Jock is also sitting up with a drip in his arm. All his clothes have been removed and he is stick thin in his gown. He's obviously had a shower as well and he smells of something noxious.

"Look at you all bonnie in your dressing gown. Are they burning your clothes as well?"

"I think they've thrown them in the bin. Have they burnt yours?"

"Aye, They said I had lice. Body lice and head lice."

That explains the strange smell.

"I've no' got any clothes now. I don't know what I'll do when I leave here."

"Jock, the last thing you need to worry about is your clothes. We'll get you a new set. In fact we'll get you several new sets. Just you concentrate on getting better."

"Thanks Shona." He is silent for a few seconds and then tears fill his eyes. "What am I going to do without Maggie?"

"Jock, you need to look after yourself for a while. We'll all miss Maggie. She was the station dog as much as yours."

"I know, but it's hard."

She squeezes his hand and kisses his cheek. "I'll be back later."

She hears a voice behind her. "I turn my back for a minute and you're kissing other men." There's smile in his voice.

Jock wipes away his tears with a calloused hand. "If I was a couple of years younger you'd have a fight on your hands," says Jock. "You look after her now," he adds.

"I fully intend to Jock. You needn't worry about that." Douglas hands Shona the bag with her clothes and shakes Jock's hand. "You look after yourself as well."

Shona gets dressed and asks a passing nurse about the baby.

"She's being treated for severe dehydration. I think she's also hungry. She's a good pair of lungs on her though. She's telling the world what she thinks of it, and it's treatment."

Shona tries for a half smile. "Give me a ring and let me know how she's doing."

"Will do. Don't you fret, she'll be well looked after."

Shona isn't sure what she should do next. She returns to her cubicle and waits. A doctor, who looks about fourteen, arrives and tells her she has been pronounced fit and is free to go.

"If you've had a tetanus injection that is," he says.

Shona isn't sure so she's given a booster. Compared to the travails of the last couple of days, the thought of an injection is nothing.

Douglas has arranged for his mother to pick them up and take them to Bell Street Station.

"You need to go home to the kids, Douglas. I don't want them worrying," says Shona.

"They're fine. In fact they love their big cousin so much they probably haven't even missed me. Besides my car is at the station and you don't have a car."

"I'm hoping that they'll find it in the compound. I want my phone and handbag if they're still there."

"I'm sure a whole squadron of coppers will be able to sort it out."

49

The whole station is overjoyed to see her. Everyone from the desk sergeant to Mo the cleaner, shakes her hand or envelopes her in a huge hug. There is a mahoosive bouquet of flowers in her office.

"That's from us all, Ma'am," says Peter. "We were that worried about you. It's good to see you back and in the office."

"I'll even be glad to hear you bollocking me again," says Roy.

Everyone laughs.

The boss calls her into his office. "What is it with you McKenzie? You can't seem to undertake a case without someone getting hurt and ending up in hospital. This time you surpassed yourself. Getting yourself abducted is a feat no other officer has ever managed. It will go down in the annals of station history."

"Sorry, Sir." She stops. She could swear the Chief is smiling. At least she thinks that's what it is.

"You did well in this case, Shona. I'm proud of you. Well done. I'm glad you're okay. I have some good news for you. PIRC have decided that there is no blame to be attached to your department regarding the explosives."

Then she is once more looking at his bald head.

"Thank you, Sir." She walks out of his office bemused.

She asks Nina if she will get her some sort of roll from the canteen. "All I've eaten since yesterday lunch time is a bit of bread and a slice of cheese. I gave my apple to Jock, who I think in turn gave it to Elspeth."

She turns to Peter. "Is our suspect here or is he under guard in Ninewells Hospital?"

"He's calmed down and they brought him here. We've a couple of bobbies standing guard in case the giant wakes up again."

"Get them to bring him to an interview room. Do we know his name?"

"No' as far as I've heard."

"Get the duty Solicitor. I don't want to speak to him without a witness."

The suspect stares straight ahead, eyes vacant. Shona has to do the usual preliminaries.

"Interview with..." She pauses. "Sir, I need your name."

The suspect doesn't so much as move his eyes.

"Sir, I am Detective Inspector Shona McKenzie. Can you tell me your name please."

No response.

Shona gives it up for the minute and says, "Interview with unnamed suspect blah, blah, blah. "

"How am I meant to represent my client when he won't speak?" says Stephen Slater, the solicitor who's covering those who can't afford a decent lawyer. Shona is sure it took him twenty years to get through Law school as he's in his mid forties and only just started practicing.

"I've no idea. How about you think about that for a wee while. You can do it whist I'm questioning him."

Slater looks perplexed. Shona thinks he's as loopy as his client."

"Sir, do you know why you were arrested?"

Nothing.

"Sir you have been arrested for the abduction and murder of four men and one woman."

Nothing.

"You mutilated them by carving a cross on their chest. Why did you do it?"

Just as Shona is thinking the whole thing is futile the man sits up straight and appears to grow in stature. His powerful voice booms out.

"I am the Great High Priest, the chosen one of God. Those who have elected to defile themselves and the world have been cleansed. They have been slain in line with God's command to me. They will perish in the fires of hell."

Before they can draw a breath to respond the man slumps down in his chair. He licks his lips and his eyes are furtive. His voice low and eerie he says, "They will be welcomed into my kingdom of darkness. No longer free to roam the earth. I have claimed my children." The suspect stands and continues, "They are mine and I have reclaimed them. Branded by the sword of the enemy, they are now home."

Peter and a couple of burly coppers haul him back into the chair.

A couple of minutes pass before Shona finds her voice. "Take him back to the cells. I'm off to ring Carstairs."

"A prison for nutjobs. It's the best place for him, Ma'am."

Shona leaves Peter to have the last word. He has summed it up beautifully.

Nina returns from the canteen with Doreen in tow. "You need something more than a bacon roll Shona. From what I hear you've been through a right turmoil." She presents Shona with a plate heaped with sausage bacon, egg, lorne sausage, black pudding, dumpling and a couple of fried eggs. "It's on the house. I'm sure Police Scotland can bear the cost given everything you

do for them."
Shona hugs her. It's a day for hugs.

All Shona wants to do is go home and sleep. However, duty demands she do another interview. This time with the purple dinosaur.

This is possibly the most pleasing interview Shona has ever done.

"Barnabas James-Hunter we are arresting you for abduction and plagium. You do not have to say anything, but it may harm your defence if you do not mention when questioned something, which you later rely on in court. Anything you do say may be given in evidence."

"What? You can't do that."

"I just did. Just so we're clear, as you're not Scottish. Plagium means theft of a child."

"I did no such thing…"

"Sergeant Johnston take our prisoner back to the cells." She turns back to Barney. "You can argue the toss about that one with the Sherriff when you come before him in the morning."

She is in her office, coming to the end of all the paperwork, when the phone rings.
"It's Jacqueline, the senior charge nurse from Accident and Emergency. I thought you'd like to know your wee bairn is doing well. She's off the drip and drinking from a bottle."
"Thanks for letting me know."

"You're welcome. One more thing, we've decided to call her Shona."

WENDY H. JONES

Wendy H. Jones lives in Dundee, Scotland, and her police procedural series featuring Detective Inspector Shona McKenzie, is set in Dundee.

Wendy, who is a committed Christian, has led a varied and adventurous life. Her love for adventure led to her joining the Royal Navy to undertake nurse training. After six years in the Navy she joined the Army where she served as an Officer for a further 17 years. This took her all over the world including the Middle East and the Far East. Much of her spare time is now spent travelling around the UK, and lands much further afield.

As well as nursing Wendy also worked for many years in Academia. This led to publication in academic textbooks and journals. Killer's Cross is the third book in the Shona McKenzie series.

THE DI SHONA McKENZIE MYSTERIES

Killer's Countdown
Killer's Craft
Killer's Cross

FIND OUT MORE

Website: http://www.wendyhjones.com

Full list of links: http://about.me/WendyHJones

Twitter: https://twitter.com/WendyHJones

Photographs of the places mentioned in the book can be found at: http://www.pinterest.com/wjones64/my-dundee/

Made in the USA
Charleston, SC
16 December 2015